EM

"I can't leave ... *I won't."*

Caitlin dashed the tears from her eyes. "They're my daughters and I love them. Don't you understand? There has to be a way to solve this."

"We're not getting on a plane without both these babies," Matt said, turning to the man who was in charge of issuing visas.

"I'm not the bad guy here." Henry Hudson threw up his hands. "These aren't my rules, but I have to follow them." He paused and narrowed his eyes. "Okay, Elizabeth Kane, what sneaky little plan do you have up your sleeve?"

"Elizabeth?" Caitlin asked, her heart racing as she turned to the director of the adoption agency.

"All right. Caitlin's application to adopt one child as a single mom was approved months ago, but you see, since then her circumstances have changed."

The director beamed. "Caitlin got married. She is now…ta-da…Mrs. Matt MacAllister."

Dear Reader,

It's that time of year again…for decking the halls, trimming the tree…and sitting by the crackling fire with a good book. And we at Silhouette have just the one to start you off—Joan Elliott Pickart's *The Marrying MacAllister,* the next offering in her series, THE BABY BET: MACALLISTER'S GIFTS. When a prospective single mother out to adopt one baby finds herself unable to choose between two orphaned sisters, she is distressed, until the perfect solution appears: marry handsome fellow traveler and renowned single guy Matt MacAllister! Your heart will melt along with his resolve.

MONTANA MAVERICKS: THE KINGSLEYS concludes with *Sweet Talk* by Jackie Merritt. When the beloved town veterinarian—and trauma survivor—is captivated by the town's fire chief, she tries to suppress her feelings. But the rugged hero is determined to make her his. Reader favorite Annette Broadrick continues her SECRET SISTERS series with *Too Tough To Tame.* A woman out to avenge the harm done to her family paints a portrait of her nemesis—which only serves to bring the two of them together. In *His Defender,* Stella Bagwell offers another MEN OF THE WEST book, in which a lawyer hired to defend a ranch owner winds up under his roof…and falling for his newest client! In *Make-Believe Mistletoe* by Gina Wilkins, a single female professor who has wished for an eligible bachelor for Christmas hardly thinks the grumpy but handsome man who's reluctantly offered her shelter from a storm is the answer to her prayers—at least not at first. And speaking of Christmas wishes—five-year-old twin boys have made theirs—and it all revolves around a new daddy. The candidate they have in mind? The handsome town sheriff, in *Daddy Patrol* by Sharon DeVita.

As you can see, no matter what romantic read you have in mind this holiday season, we have the book for you. Happy holidays, happy reading—and come back next month, for six new wonderful offerings from Silhouette Special Edition!

Sincerely,

Gail Chasan
Senior Editor

Please address questions and book requests to:
Silhouette Reader Service
U.S.: 3010 Walden Ave., P.O. Box 1325, Buffalo, NY 14269
Canadian: P.O. Box 609, Fort Erie, Ont. L2A 5X3

Joan Elliott Pickart

The Marrying MacAllister

Silhouette®

SPECIAL EDITION™

Published by Silhouette Books

America's Publisher of Contemporary Romance

For my nifty niece
ALIDA ELIZABETH HUNT

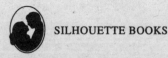

SILHOUETTE BOOKS

ISBN 0-373-24579-3

THE MARRYING MACALLISTER

Copyright © 2003 by Joan Elliott Pickart

This edition published by arrangement with Harlequin Books S.A.

Visit Silhouette at www.eHarlequin.com

Printed in U.S.A.

Books by Joan Elliott Pickart

Silhouette Special Edition

*Friends, Lovers...and
  Babies! #1011
*The Father of Her Child #1025
†Texas Dawn #1100
†Texas Baby #1141
Wife Most Wanted #1160
The Rancher and the Amnesiac
  Bride #1204
∆The Irresistible
  Mr. Sinclair #1256
∆The Most Eligible M.D. #1262
Man...Mercenary...Monarch #1303
*To a MacAllister Born #1329
*Her Little Secret #1377
Single with Twins #1405
◊The Royal MacAllister #1477
◊Tall, Dark and Irresistible #1507
◊The Marrying MacAllister #1579

*The Baby Bet
†Family Men
∆The Bachelor Bet
◊The Baby Bet: MacAllister's Gifts

Silhouette Desire

*Angels and Elves #961
Apache Dream Bride #999
†Texas Moon #1051
†Texas Glory #1088
Just My Joe #1202
∆Taming Tall, Dark Brandon #1223
*Baby: MacAllister-Made #1326
*Plain Jane MacAllister #1462

Silhouette Books

A Mother's Gift
  "Mother's Day Baby"
Body of Evidence
  "Verdict: Matrimony"
*His Secret Son
◊Party of Three
◊Crowned Hearts
  "A Wish and a Prince"

Previously published under the pseudonym Robin Elliott

Silhouette Special Edition

Rancher's Heaven #909
Mother at Heart #968

Silhouette Intimate Moments

Gauntlet Run #206

Silhouette Desire

Call It Love #213
To Have It All #237
Picture of Love #261
Pennies in the Fountain #275
Dawn's Gift #303
Brooke's Chance #323
Betting Man #344
Silver Sands #362
Lost and Found #384
Out of the Cold #440
Sophie's Attic #725
Not Just Another Perfect Wife #818
Haven's Call #859

JOAN ELLIOTT PICKART

When she isn't writing, Joan enjoys reading, gardening and attending craft shows with her young daughter, Autumn. Joan has three all-grown-up daughters and three fantastic grandchildren.

Dear Reader,

You are about to go on a trip to the enchanting land of China and you don't even have to worry about attempting to pack all your goodies into one suitcase.

I hope you enjoy reading Matt and Caitlin's story as much as I did writing it. It gave me the opportunity to relive all the wonderful memories of my own trip to Hong Kong, Nanjing and Guangzhou when I adopted my three-month-old daughter Autumn in 1995.

As writers we sometimes wiggle facts around a bit to enable our characters to have their dreams come true. I wish to make it clear that Elizabeth's solution to Caitlin and Matt's dilemma and Henry's agreeing to take part in it would never have taken place. INS would not have accepted a last-minute change in Caitlin's application under any circumstances.

But this book is fiction where fairy tales are allowed to come true.

So sit back, put your feet up and travel the sometimes bumpy road to forever love with Caitlin, Matt and two little China dolls who will hopefully steal your heart.

Warmest regards,

Joan Elliott Pickart

Chapter One

"I warned you, MacAllister, but you refused to listen. Now? I'm going to punch your ticket."

Matt MacAllister glared at his longtime friend, Bud Mathis, who sat behind the desk in a masculinely decorated office. Matt was opposite the desk in a comfortable chair, one ankle propped on his other knee.

"Come on, Bud. Give me a break. Cut me some slack here."

"It's Dr. Mathis to you at the moment," Bud said, crossing his arms over his chest. "I already gave you a second chance. I told you a month ago that I'd hold off on faxing my report on your yearly physical to the board of directors at the hospital for thirty days to give you an opportunity to quit working such long hours, get proper rest, eat decently and on the list goes.

"Did you utilize that month to your advantage? Nope. You still have high blood pressure that is the cause of your frequent headaches, you're suffering from exhaustion and your ulcer is on the warpath."

"Being the public-relations director at Mercy Hospital is not a lightweight position, Bud," Matt said, dropping his foot to the floor. "Situations occur that simply can't be postponed because my doctor says I need to go home and take a nap."

"I heard this spiel a month ago. So cork it. I'm not giving you a clean bill of health so you can continue as you are. I am, in fact, going to inform the board that you're to take a medical leave for a minimum of a month and perhaps even longer."

Matt lunged to his feet. "Now wait just a damn minute."

"Sit," Bud said, meeting Matt glare for glare.

Matt muttered an earthy expletive, then slouched back onto the chair, his eyebrows knitted in a frown.

"I'll give you one week," Bud went on, "to bring the attorney the hospital keeps on retainer up to date on pending files, and you can use those same days to find a replacement to attend the fund-raising events that you said are scheduled on your calendar. After that, you're not to put one foot inside the hospital until you've cleared it through me.''

"Ah, man," Matt said, dragging one hand through his thick, auburn hair. "Some friend you are. I'll go nuts just sitting around. And if you tell me to go fishing or take up bridge I'll deck you.''

"I don't want you to even be here in Ventura," Bud said, "because you'll cheat, be on the phone every other minute to the attorney covering your spot.

"Marsha and I were talking about you last night, Matt. I told her it would be a very safe bet that you'd flunk your physical today. We came up with what we feel is a terrific solution to your situation.''

"I bet you have," Matt said, rolling his eyes heavenward.

"Just listen…and keep an open mind. You know that Marsha and I have spent months completing the paperwork to adopt a baby girl from China.''

"Of course I know that. I'm going to be her godfather.''

"Yes, you are." Bud nodded. "Well, the adoption agency says the match pictures are on the way. It's finally happening, Matt. We're going to fly to the other side of the world and bring home our little miracle.''

Matt smiled. "No joke? That's great. I'm really

happy for you and Marsha.'' He paused and frowned again. ''But I don't have a clue as to what this has to do with your not allowing me to work at the hospital for the next month.''

''It's very simple. Marsha and I want you to come with us on the trip to China.''

''What?''

''It's perfect, don't you see?'' Bud said, flinging out his arms. ''If you're in China you sure can't pop into Mercy Hospital when no one is looking, nor pick up the phone to check on things every two seconds.

''You won't be under any stress during the trip because *you're* not the one who will be tending to a new member of the family. That awesome task is delegated to those of us in our group who are adopting the little ones.''

''But...''

''Hear me out.'' Bud raised one hand. ''We'll be over there for about two weeks as there are legal matters to attend to. However, the Chinese government schedules one meeting a day, leaving foreign visitors plenty of time to tour and spend money. To top it off, you'll be traveling with your own physician...me...and I intend to keep an eagle eye on you. Like I said...it's perfect.''

''It's nuts, that's what it is. You plan to just inform the adoption agency that a friend of yours is going to tag along for the ride? Yeah, right.''

"Yeah, you *are* right," Bud said, appearing extremely pleased with himself. "That's exactly what Marsha and I would do. One of the couples of the five families in our group is bringing the new grandparents along, and the one single mom has been advised to have a friend with her to help with luggage and what have you because there are no bellhops or redcaps in China.

"All the agency needs to know within the next few days is how many people are actually going so they can make arrangements."

"Oh," Matt said.

"Look, don't give me an answer now, but promise me you'll think about it. It's a win-win situation, Matt. You can't be tempted to sneak in some work time, plus you'll be sharing a very special event with Marsha and me and meeting your new goddaughter.

"This is Monday. The match pictures are winging their way west even as we speak. On Wednesday night everyone involved is coming to our house at six-thirty for a potluck dinner to receive the pictures…God, what a moment that will be…and to get instructions on dos and don'ts while in China so we don't offend anyone over there.

"It's called a culture training meeting and your cousin Carolyn will be conducting it. Carolyn isn't going on the trip because she's pregnant, as you know. Elizabeth Kane, the director of the agency, will be accompanying us.

"All I'm asking at this point, Matt, is that you attend the potluck at our house Wednesday night, having kept an open mind about possibly joining us on this trip. What do you say? Will you come Wednesday?"

Matt sighed. "Yeah, I guess so. It can't hurt to listen, I suppose, and I'll be able to see the picture of your daughter. But China? It's not exactly around the corner, Bud."

"No, it's a long, long way from Mercy Hospital in Ventura, California, my friend, which makes it a custom-ordered place for you to travel to. Hey, it beats going fishing."

"That's a very good point," Matt said, raising a finger. "I'll be at your house Wednesday night, but I'm not promising anything."

"Fair enough," Bud said. "There's something else that you ought to consider, too. A MacAllister going on a vacation is no big deal. But a Mac-Allister who is on a doctor-ordered medical leave? That's news and you'd be kidding yourself if you thought the press wouldn't get wind of it. If you stay in Ventura you'll be hounded by reporters wanting all the details regarding your health."

"The thought of that is enough to make my ulcer go nuts," Matt said, getting to his feet. "Do they have any forks in China? I have never been able to master the use of chopsticks. It's not going to do your reputation as a doctor any good if your patient starves to death while accompanying you to a foreign country, chum.''

Bud laughed. ''You can pack a fork in your suitcase just to be on the safe side of that question.''

''This isn't sounding like a thrill a minute, Mathis,'' Matt said, heading toward the door of the office. ''Yeah, yeah, I know, it beats going fishing. I'll see you Wednesday night.'' He opened the door, then turned to look at Bud again. ''Potluck. What should I bring?''

''An attitude adjustment.''

''Hell,'' Matt said, then strode out of the office.

By Wednesday night Matt's attitude was well on its way to being adjusted.

He parked his SUV behind the last car in the row in front of the Mathises' large ranch-style house, crossed his arms on the top of the steering wheel and glowered into space.

China, here I come, he thought. The last two days had been a study in frustration as he'd started the process of bringing the hospital's attorney up to date on the pending files that needed to be brought to closure. There was no doubt in his mind that the attorney would be calling him every two seconds to double-check something, causing him to want to march back over there and do it himself.

Stress to the max, that's what it would be, and his blood pressure would probably go off the Richter scale, making it impossible to get a passing grade on Bud's crummy physical.

Did he want to go to China and starve to death because he couldn't master the use of chopsticks? No. Was he in the mood for tours and sight-seeing trips with the typical bit about ''On your left you will see…''? No. Did he feel like being surrounded by a slew of nervous new parents and babies who would no doubt wail their dismay at the sudden changes taking place in their lives? No.

Hey, he loved kids, which was a good thing since he was a MacAllister and was in proximity to the diaper brigade in vast numbers at every family gathering. But the scenario with *these* babies and *these* parents was far from the norm, and the new mom and dad's tension would be sensed by the munchkin and they'd all be wrecks.

Nope, he didn't want to go to China with this group, Matt thought as he rang the doorbell, but the opportunity was there and it certainly would put distance between himself and the attorney from hell. So be it.

The front door opened and a smiling Marsha Mathis greeted Matt. She was a tall, attractive blonde in her early thirties, who immediately kissed Matt on the cheek, then slipped one arm through one of his.

"I'll give you a quick introduction to everyone, Matt," Marsha said, "but if no one remembers your name the first time around don't take it personally, because we are coming unglued. Carolyn arrived just moments before you did and she's about to pass out the match pictures. I can hardly believe this is really happening after all these months."

"I'm very happy for you and Bud. That little lady waiting for you in China is a fortunate kiddo to be getting parents like you two."

"Oh, we're the ones who are counting our blessings," Marsha said as they entered a large family room beyond the living room. "Everyone, this is Matt MacAllister, who will hopefully be accompanying us on the trip. He's Carolyn's cousin-in-law, or some such thing."

"Hello, Matt," Carolyn said, smiling at him from across the room.

"Hi, Carolyn," Matt said. "How's Ryan?"

"Super."

"Okay, I'll make this fast," Marsha said, "so we can get our match pictures. Matt, that couple on the love seat is…"

Within seconds Matt gave up even comprehending what Marsha was saying, let alone being able to remember the names of the dozen-plus people, because she was rattling them off so fast it was a blur of sound. He just smiled and nodded, then nodded some more.

"And last but not least," Marsha said, "is our single mommy, Caitlin Cunningham. That's it. Find a place to sit, Matt." She hurried across the room to settle on a chair next to Bud and grab his hand.

Caitlin Cunningham, Matt mused, still looking at her where she was sitting on the raised hearth in front of the fireplace. *That* name belonging to *that* woman was now etched indelibly in his mind.

She was absolutely lovely.

With short, curly dark hair, delicate features and the biggest, most expressive eyes he'd ever seen, combined with a slender figure clad in pale blue slacks and a very feminine flowered top, Caitlin Cunningham was, indeed, worth remembering.

Matt made his way across the room and settled onto the hearth about three feet away from Caitlin, whose gaze was riveted on Carolyn. He slid a glance at Caitlin, and realized that she was clutching her hands so tightly beneath her chin that her knuckles were white. She drew a shuddering breath as Carolyn opened a large envelope and removed five envelopes containing the match pictures.

"The big moment has arrived, huh?" Matt said, directing his statement toward Caitlin.

She did not respond, nor give any indication that she had even heard him.

Way to go, MacAllister, Matt thought. He'd sure knocked her out with his good looks and charm. She was speechless with awe. Yeah, right.

He could tear off all his clothes and do a hip-swiveling dance worthy of a male stripper and he seriously doubted if Caitlin Cunningham would even notice.

Well, maybe he was being too hard on himself. After all, Ms. Cunningham was about to see a picture of her new child for the very first time. Nobody could compete with *that*.

Matt continued to scrutinize Caitlin out of the corner of his eye while being vaguely aware of the sound of excited reactions as well as sniffles in the background as Carolyn passed out the envelopes.

Carolyn moved to where Caitlin was sitting and gave her one of the coveted envelopes.

"Congratulations, Mother," Carolyn said, smiling.

With a trembling hand Caitlin took the envelope from Carolyn.

"Thank you, Carolyn," Caitlin said softly. "I... Thank you."

"Open the envelope." Carolyn laughed. "Staring at it like that isn't going to give you your first glimpse of your daughter. Okay, off I go. This is such fun."

"Well," Caitlin said, now gripping the envelope with both hands. "My daughter's picture is in here.

Oh, my goodness, *my daughter's picture is in this envelope*. This is wonderful and terrifying and…oh dear.'.'

Matt scooted about a foot closer to Caitlin on the hearth.

''Do you need some help opening that?''

''Aakk,'' Caitlin said, her head snapping around. ''Who are you?''

''Matt MacAllister,'' he said, frowning. ''Marsha introduced me when I came in. Remember? No, I guess you don't. This is quite a moment in your life. Go ahead. Say hello to your daughter.''

''Yes, yes, I'm going to do that,'' Caitlin said, nodding jerkily. ''Right now.'' She slid a fingertip under the flap of the envelope, lifted it, hesitated, then reached inside and took out two pictures. A lovely smile instantly formed on her lips and her eyes filled with tears. ''Oh, look at her. Just look at her. She's the most beautiful baby I've ever seen. My daughter. This is my baby.''

Matt craned his neck with the hope of getting a peek at the photographs but couldn't see them. He moved closer to Caitlin, just as she turned the pictures over to read what was written on the back.

''She's… Oh, I've forgotten every bit of math I've ever known. Okay, let's see. She's six months and…two, three…yes, six months and four days old.'' She looked at Matt. ''Isn't she gorgeous?''

Matt chuckled. "I'm sure she is, but I haven't seen her yet."

"Oh," Caitlin said, turning the photos back over and holding them side by side for Matt to see. "Look, here she is."

A funny little sensation of warmth seemed to tip-toe around and through Matt's heart as he studied the pictures of the baby.

She had black hair that was sticking up in all directions, dark almond-shaped eyes that were staring right at the camera, a rosebud mouth and in both shots she was scowling with not even a hint of a smile. In one picture she was wearing a pink blanket sleeper and in another a faded red one.

Matt's palms actually began to tingle as he had the irrational urge to reach out, lift the baby from the photograph and nestle her close, hold her tight, tell her everything was going to be just fine.

"She's…" He cleared his throat. "She's a heart-stealer, Caitlin. Congratulations. Your daughter is…well, she's really something. What are you going to name her?"

"I can't decide between Mackenzie and Madison," Caitlin said, gazing at the pictures again. "I think I'll wait until I actually hold her in my arms before I pick which one is right for her."

"Is everybody happy?" Carolyn said from across the room.

A chorus of affirmative replies filled the air.

"Some of you may have gotten more than one picture of your daughter," Carolyn went on. "There's never any rhyme or reason to what they send. I know you could spend the rest of the evening just gazing at those photos, but we have a lot to cover. Marsha, why don't we have our potluck supper, then we can get down to business. Let's take a few minutes to share the photographs with everyone before dinner."

"Okay," Marsha said, getting to her feet. "Matt, come see the picture of your goddaughter. She's eleven months old and she's standing alone in this photo. She's fantastic. Oh, I'm going to cry again."

Matt crossed the room and grinned when he saw the picture of Marsha and Bud's baby. She was wearing a dress that was much too large for her, was obviously not very steady on her feet, as she was holding her arms straight out at her sides, but had a broad smile on her face as though she knew that standing alone was a very big deal. She had a little fluff of dark hair on the top of her head and her smile revealed four teeth—two on the top and two on the bottom.

"Dynamite," Matt said, laughing. "You two better get your track shoes ready. This little lady is about to conquer the challenge of walking."

"Isn't her hair funny?" Bud said. "I love it. Just one wild plop on the top of her head. Hey, Grace,

I'm your daddy. Grace Marsha Mathis. How's that, Matt?''

''Perfect,'' Matt said. ''Grace. That's nice. I like it. Caitlin is still undecided between naming her baby Mackenzie or Madison.''

''Oh?'' Marsha said, raising her eyebrows. ''Caitlin told you that?''

''Well, yeah, I was sitting right there and asked her what she was going to name her and… Marsha, don't start your matchmaking thing. Okay?'' Matt rolled his eyes heavenward. ''I almost didn't survive that bit the last time you did it. Concentrate on Grace Marsha Mathis and forget about me.''

''What I want to know, ole chum,'' Bud said, ''is whether or not you've made up your mind about going to China with us.''

''Count me in. I wouldn't miss it for the world. When do we leave?''

''I'm not certain. Carolyn may announce the date after dinner.''

''Dinner,'' Marsha said. ''That's what I'm supposed to be doing.''

Marsha rushed off and Caitlin followed her to help put the potluck dishes on the dining-room table. The pictures of the babies were passed around, and Matt made no attempt to curb his smile as he looked at each one. They ranged in age from four months to two years.

"What made you decide to go with us on this trip?" Bud asked Matt.

"A lamebrain attorney. Well, that was the reason when I arrived here tonight. But now? This whole thing is awesome, Bud. Families are being created, kids are going to be brought out of crowded orphanages into loving homes and...I want to be there when you see Grace for the first time and Caitlin holds Mackenzie or Madison, whichever name she decides on and...I'm honestly looking forward to going on this journey. I'm...I'm honored to be included."

Bud nodded. "We're glad you're going to be with us, sharing it all." He paused. "I am now going to chat—not gossip—chat with you. Caitlin works with Marsha at the fashion magazine. Marsha is the assistant editor, as you know, and Caitlin is a copywriter. A very talented one, as a matter of fact.

"The way Marsha tells it, Caitlin wanted to hear every detail of what we were discovering about adopting from China since Marsha is unable to have kids. The Chinese government allows single women to adopt and Caitlin decided it was the perfect answer for her as well."

"Why?"

"That we don't know." Bud shrugged. "She just said that she hoped her approval came through at the same time as ours so we'd be traveling together to get our daughters. I believe a girlfriend of Caitlin's is going with her to help out, like the agency suggested for single moms. The friend must have been busy tonight.''

"Interesting," Matt said. "I mean, hey, Caitlin is a lovely young woman. Why isn't she married and having a slew of kids herself? Why is she going the single-mom route?''

"Don't have a clue," Bud said. "I'm hungry.''

"Who's hungry?" Marsha called from the doorway.

"I swear, my wife can read my mind, which is a scary thought at times.''

Matt managed to snag the chair next to Caitlin, and Marsha and Bud sat across from them. The pictures were placed carefully in front of plates around the table. The food was delicious, the conversation centered on babies and the eagerly anticipated journey to the other side of the world.

"Attention, attention," Carolyn said as a three-layer chocolate cake was being served for dessert. "I'll talk so I won't be tempted to indulge in that chocolate delight. Question. Has there been any change in the number of people going along with you?''

"Yes," Caitlin said. "My girlfriend who was to accompany me to help with the luggage and what have you broke her ankle while in-line skating with her son. My mother and stepfather live in Italy and my stepfather is ill, making it impossible for my mother to leave him right now. Other friends can't get vacation time on such short notice. So, I'm on my own.''

''We'll all help you, Caitlin,'' Bud said. ''In fact, we're adding Matt to the list of who is going and he'll be free to assist you with your luggage. Right, Matt?''

''Sure,'' Matt said. ''No problem.''

''All things should be so easily solved.'' Carolyn laughed. ''Okay, then, I have the final count so reservations will be made. You'll be called just as soon as everything is arranged and we have a date of departure. It will be soon, I promise. Matt, is your passport current?''

''Yes, ma'am. I'm ready to rock and roll.''

''Excellent.'' Carolyn paused. ''Finish your sinful dessert while I get the information packets I want to pass out to you.''

''I appreciate your willingness to help me with my luggage, Matt,'' Caitlin said.

''It will be my pleasure,'' he said, smiling at her. ''I'll just be hanging around tickling babies and taking in the sights.''

Caitlin frowned. ''I guess I don't quite understand why you're going on this trip. Have you always wanted to travel to China and the opportunity presented itself?''

''Well, not exactly.''

"Before Matt says something that will make his nose grow," Bud said, "I'm squealing on him. As his physician I ordered him to stay away from his job as public-relations director at Mercy Hospital for a month because he's been working far too many hours for far too long. It was go to China with us, or be sent to his room for being a naughty boy."

"Thank you, Dr. Mouth Mathis," Matt said dryly.

"Well, it's true," Marsha said. "Work, work, work, that's all you do, Matt. This trip is just what the doctor, my sweet patootie, ordered."

"Whatever." Matt chuckled. "I happen to like my job, you know."

"More than anything else," Marsha retorted. "But we gotcha good, MacAllister. You can't drop by the hospital when you're hiking around China."

Caitlin laughed along with everyone else who had heard the conversation, but she sighed inwardly.

Oh, yes, she thought, the same old story. Here was another handsome and intelligent man who was pleasant to be with, but who was focused on his career above everything else. History seemed to repeat itself time and again for as long as she could remember. Men crossed her path who had priorities at opposite poles from hers. Well, hello and goodbye to Mr. Matt MacAllister of *the* MacAllisters of Ventura. So be it.

"Is something wrong, Caitlin?" Matt said. "You look so serious all of a sudden."

"What? Oh. No. Nothing is wrong, Matt." She smiled. "I was just doing a bit of reality check time." She picked up the pictures of her daughter and gazed at them. "But I'm fine now. We're going to be a terrific team, my daughter and I. Just the two of us."

The woman on the other side of Caitlin spoke to her, causing her to turn away from Matt. He looked at her delicate fingers as they held the photographs of the baby Caitlin would name either Mackenzie or Madison.

We're going to be a terrific team, my daughter and I. Just the two of us.

Caitlin's words echoed in Matt's mind and he frowned.

Why? he wondered. Why was an extremely attractive, intelligent, I-have-a-lot-to-offer woman like Caitlin Cunningham seemingly determined to be a single mother, making no room in her life for a husband for herself, a father for that adorable baby girl?

Had Caitlin been deeply hurt by a man in the past? Whoa. He didn't like the idea of that, not one little bit.

Or…like Marsha, was Caitlin unable to have

children and felt that no man would want to marry her because of that?

Or... Hell, he didn't know.

She was an enigma, the lovely Ms. Cunningham, and for reasons he couldn't begin to fathom he wanted to unravel the mysteries, the secrets, surrounding her, discover who she really was, and why she had chosen the path leading to China and the baby who was waiting for her there.

Chapter Two

Everyone pitched in to clear away the dishes, and packed up their own containers to take home. Paper and pens were then produced to take notes on what Carolyn was going to say regarding the trip to China. She passed out a packet of papers.

"The information on these sheets," Carolyn said from where she sat at the head of the table, "touches on the high spots of what I'm going to tell you." She laughed. "Experience has shown that our new moms and dads can get a bit spacey on the night they receive their match pictures, so we put some of the data in print for you to read later."

Everyone laughed and Caitlin smiled at Matt, who was still sitting next to her.

"Do I look spacey to you?" she said.

She looked pretty as a picture, Matt thought, staring directly into her eyes.

"You're over the top," he said, smiling. "Totally zoned."

"I'm sorry I asked," Caitlin said, matching his smile.

"Fear not, new mommy. I'll take plenty of notes that will be at your disposal. Those plus the handout from Carolyn ought to cover it for you."

"Thank you, sir," Caitlin said, then redirected her attention to Carolyn.

Good grief, Caitlin thought, Matt MacAllister was so ruggedly handsome it was sinful. That auburn hair of his was a rich, yummy color like, well, like an Irish setter. And those brown eyes of his. Gracious, they were like fathomless pools of…of fudge sauce and… Oh, for Pete's sake, this was silly. Matt reminded her of a dog with eyes the color of an ice-cream topping? That was a rather bizarre description.

But there was no getting around the fact that Matt would turn women's heads whenever he entered the room. He was tall and well built with wide shoulders and long, muscular legs. He moved with an easy grace, like an athlete, a man who was comfortable in his own body.

He was charming, intelligent, had a way of listening that made a person feel very special and important. And when he looked directly into her eyes there was no ignoring that she felt a funny little flutter slither down her spine. Yes, masculinity personified was the drop-dead gorgeous Mr. MacAllister.

He was also one of the multitudes who was focused on his career to the exclusion of everything else in his life. No one was perfect and that was Matt's flaw, his glaring glitch. And she had no intention of allowing all his other attributes to make her forget it, not for one little second.

"Okay, first up," Carolyn said. "We ask that you don't wear jeans while in China. I know that must sound picky, but we're going into a country with a different culture than ours and we want to exhibit the respect due our hosts."

"But we can wear slacks?" Marsha asked.

"Yes," Carolyn said. "In any material other than denim."

"I'm writing this down," Matt said.

"Go for it." Caitlin laughed softly.

"You'll be spending one night in Hong Kong," Carolyn went on, "which we have found helps the jet-lag problem at least a little bit. The flight to Hong Kong is fifteen hours nonstop, so it's imperative that you get up, walk around the airplane and drink lots of water during the flight.

"After the night in Hong Kong you'll fly into Nanjing, China, and you'll be staying at a lovely hotel there. Cribs will be placed in each of your rooms for the babies."

"Oh-h-h," a woman named Jane said, "a crib."

Her husband Bill chuckled. "This is going to be a long, weepy trip, no doubt about it."

"Well, we've waited a long time to need a baby crib, honey," Jane said, sniffling.

"I know, sweetheart," he said, then kissed her on the forehead.

And they're sharing it all, together, every precious moment of it, Caitlin thought. No, no, she wasn't going to go there, wouldn't dwell on the fact that she was the only single mother making this journey. She'd thought and prayed for many months before making the decision to adopt a baby and it was right for her, just as it stood. This was the way she wanted it. This was the way it was going to be.

"Feel free to get all dewy-eyed about the crib in the room," Matt whispered to Caitlin. "Everyone else seems to be."

"I'm holding myself back. I'm saving up for when my daughter is *in* that crib."

"Good idea."

"On page two of your packet," Carolyn said, "is a list of suggested things to take for your baby. You will each be allowed one...I repeat...one suitcase. The laundry service in the hotels you'll be staying in is excellent, but you'll get tired of wearing the same clothes over and over. You're packing for your baby with your things tucked around the edges of that one suitcase.''

''This I've got to see,'' a man named Fred said, laughing. ''Sally takes at least five suitcases for a weekend in San Francisco. One suitcase for a two-week stay in China? And the majority of the space is for our daughter? This is going to be a hoot.''

''Hush, Fred,'' Sally said. ''I'll manage just fine, you'll see.''

''Yeah, right,'' Fred said, shaking his head and grinning.

Lots of diapers, Matt wrote on the paper in front of him.

''There are instructions on your sheets,'' Carolyn said, ''about formula and how you'll need to cut it down with water because the babies aren't used to having such rich, nourishing food on a regular basis. You're going to be easing them into it slowly so they don't get tummyaches.

''As far as your tummies, you will be consuming some of the most delicious food you've ever eaten.''

''Do they have forks in China?'' Matt asked, causing Bud to hoot with laughter.

''Yes, they have forks, Matt,'' Carolyn said. ''They're used to fumble-fingered Westerners where you'll be staying and will provide you with utensils you're accustomed to.''

''That's very comforting,'' Matt said.

''Oh, before I forget,'' Carolyn added. ''The salt and pepper shakers are reversed from ours. Pepper has the big holes, salt the small ones. Write that down so that you don't ruin the fantastic food I'm raving about.''

''Write that down,'' Caitlin said, tapping the paper in front of Matt.

''Yes, ma'am,'' he said. ''I'm on it, ma'am.''

''You'll be in Nanjing about a week,'' Carolyn said, ''then you'll fly into Guangzhou, where our American consulate is located and the visas are issued for the babies. The adoptions will be final before you leave China and you won't have to readopt through our courts here when you get back.''

A buzz of conversation began around the table at that exciting news.

''This is all very interesting,'' Matt said, nodding. ''Fascinating. Just think, Caitlin, Madison or MacKenzie, whoever she turns out to be, will be your legal daughter when you two step onto U.S. of A. soil again. That's pretty awesome, don't you… Uh-oh, the crib didn't get to you, but this one did.''

''Ignore me,'' Caitlin said, flapping a hand in front of her tear-filled eyes. ''It's just the thought of leaving here as...as me, and returning as a mother with a daughter and...oh dear.''

Matt put one arm around Caitlin's shoulders.

''Tissue alert,'' he yelled. ''We need a tissue here. Marsha, didn't I see you go get a box?''

''Here it is,'' someone said, shoving it across the table. ''The container was full when Marsha brought it out here and it's half-empty already. We're all a mess.''

''You're all delightfully normal,'' Carolyn said, smiling. ''Be certain you have tissues with you for that moment when you see and hold those babies for the first time.''

''Oh-h-h,'' a woman wailed, and the tissue box went back in the direction it had come from.

''Okay now?'' Matt said, his arm still encircling Caitlin's shoulders.

She was so delicate, he thought, and warm and feminine. He'd like to pull her close, nestle her against his chest, sift his fingers through those silky black curls, then tip her chin up, lower his lips to hers and...

''I'm fine.'' Caitlin straightened her shoulders with the hope that Matt would get the hint that he should remove his arm. Now. Right now. Because it was such a strong arm, yet he was holding her so gently, so protectively. And it was such a warm arm, the heat seeming to suffuse her was now thrumming deep and low within her and... This would never do. No. Matt had to move that arm. "You can have your arm back."

"What?" Matt said. "Oh. Sure." He slowly eased his arm away from Caitlin's shoulders.

"In Guangzhou," Carolyn said, snapping everyone back to attention, "you'll be at the White Swan Hotel, which is a five-star establishment and the one where visiting dignitaries stay. It is incredibly beautiful. I'm not going to give you any more hints about it because I want you to be surprised when you get there."

Carolyn went on for another half hour with various information, answered questions, said she would be available up until the time they left if more thoughts came to them, then promised to call each of them as soon as the departure date was set.

"It will be soon," she said. "Dr. Yang, our liaison in China, said your daughters are eager for you to arrive and take them home." She laughed. "Oops. Where did that tissue box go?"

Excitement was buzzing through the air as everyone continued to chatter, then a few said it was time to go as tomorrow was a workday.

"We've got to get a crib, Bud," Marsha said, "and a changing table and… Goodness, we have a lot to do before we leave."

"Plus I have to warn the two doctors who are going to cover my practice that they are on red-alert standby as of now," Bud said. "It's ironic, isn't it? After all these months of paperwork, then waiting, then more paperwork, then waiting, and waiting and waiting, we're going to be dashing around like crazy at the last second. I just may sleep during that entire fifteen-hour flight.''

"Color me dumb," Matt said, "but why aren't you more prepared as far as equipment goes? I mean, you don't even have a crib set up yet.''

"Well, you see, Matt," Marsha said, "when you fill out the papers, you give the officials in Beijing an age range of a child you'd be willing to adopt. In our case we said newborn to three years old. We didn't know until tonight that Grace is eleven months and will need a crib.''

"Oh, I see," Matt said. "That makes sense now.'' He looked at Caitlin. "What about you, Caitlin? Are you prepared for Mackenzie or Madison?''

"No. I painted her room pale yellow and hung yellow curtains with a bunch of bunnies as the border print. I got a white dresser and matching rocking chair and bookcase for toys, but I don't have a crib. I also put newborn to three years on that form, so I didn't know if I'd need a crib or a toddler bed. I'm thrilled to pieces that Miss M. is so young. Six months and four days.''

"We're ecstatic that Grace is only eleven months old, too," Marsha said. "We'll get to witness so many things that she does for the first time.''

''Yeah,'' Bud said, laughing, ''like leading us on a merry chase when she takes off at a run after mastering the walking bit.''

''Tomorrow evening we go shopping for a crib and changing table,'' Marsha said firmly. ''Then come home and I'll watch you put them together, Bud.''

''That's usually how those things go,'' he said.

''How about you, Caitlin?'' Matt asked. ''Could you use some help assembling your stuff?''

''Oh, I couldn't ask you to do that, Matt. You've already gotten roped into hauling my luggage around once my arms are full of baby.''

''Believe me, I don't mind giving you a hand. Thanks to Bud, who used to be my friend, I have all my evenings free. I'm accustomed to putting in those hours at the hospital. You'd be doing me a favor by getting me out of the house, because I've forgotten how to turn on my television set.''

''Well,'' Caitlin said slowly.

''It's perfect, Caitlin,'' Marsha said. ''I'd suggest that the four of us go shopping together, but we never know what time Bud will get home. You two just go ahead and make your own plans. Oh, jeez, I'm supposed to be doing my hostess duties and seeing everyone to the door.'' She got to her feet. ''Wait, wait, Sally and Fred. Give me a chance to be polite. Bud, get off your tush and come with me to execute socially acceptable behavior.''

''Whatever,'' Bud said, rising.

''Listen, try this idea,'' Matt said to Caitlin as Bud followed Marsha to the front door. ''We go out for pizza, shop for baby stuff, then go to your place and I'll put everything together. Does that work for you?''

Caitlin frowned. ''I don't think the big cartons that equipment comes in will fit in my car.''

''I have an SUV and the back seats fold down. Problem solved.''

''I don't have any tools.''

''I'll bring mine. Shall I pick you up at your place about six tomorrow night?''

''I…yes, all right. I appreciate this very much, Matt. I mean, you don't even know me and here you are willing to perform manual labor to help me complete the nursery. It's very generous of you.''

Matt picked up one of the pictures of Caitlin's daughter.

''This little lady deserves to have everything ready and waiting for her when she comes home. Man, she's cute. If she can grab hold of a person's heart when she's looking like a grumpy little old man, imagine what will happen the first time she smiles. Hey, Miss M., do you have any teeth in there to show off? How long are you going to make your mommy wait for that first smile, munchkin?''

"Her first smile," Caitlin said wistfully, then shook her head. "Don't get me started again. I think the tissue box is empty." She got to her feet. "I'll give you my address and I'll see you tomorrow night at six. Thank you again, Matt."

Matt stood. "I'm looking forward to it...very much, Caitlin."

After Matt had gotten Caitlin's address, he watched as she collected the dish she'd brought her contribution to the potluck in, hugged Carolyn, tucked the precious pictures of the baby in her purse, then bid Marsha and Bud good-night at the door. Carolyn said her goodbyes, then Matt wandered toward the front door himself.

"Need any help cleaning up?" he asked Marsha and Bud.

"No, we're fine," Bud said. "It's nice of you to give Caitlin a hand with the baby furniture, Matt."

Matt shrugged. "No biggie."

"Taking her out for pizza before you go shopping is a nice touch," Marsha said, beaming. "You're such a thoughtful guy, Matt MacAllister."

"No," he said, frowning. "I just happen to like pizza and haven't had any in a while."

"Mmm," Marsha said, batting her eyelashes at him.

"Don't start with me, Marsha. There is no room

for matchmaking in the middle of a baby boom, which is what this trip will be, so just forget it. Bud, control your wife.''

"Fat chance of that, chum," Bud said, laughing. "Wow. It just hit me. I'm going to have a wife *and* a daughter. Talk about being ganged up on by females in my own home."

"It makes my heart go pitter-patter," Marsha said. "Women rule."

"I'm outta here," Matt said, chuckling. "Thanks for a great evening. I really enjoyed it. Ah, life is full of challenges. Good night, new mommy and daddy."

"Oh-h-h, listen to that," Marsha said. "I'm going to go find a fresh box of tissues."

Caitlin propped the two pictures of the baby against the lamp on the nightstand, then wiggled into a comfortable position in the bed where she could gaze at the photographs.

"Hello, my daughter," she said, unable to curb her smile. "Are you Mackenzie, or are you Madison, Miss M.? I just don't know yet, but I will when I see you, hold you, for the first time. Will you smile then? Or make me wait for that special moment?"

She kissed the tip of one finger, then gently touched each picture.

"I wish you knew that I'll be there very soon to

get you. Maybe an angel will whisper in your ear that your mommy is coming. You won't have a daddy, sweetheart, but we'll be fine, just the two of us, you'll see.''

Caitlin turned off the light, sighed in contentment and drifted off to sleep within minutes.

Hours later Matt was still awake, staring up at the ceiling. No matter how many lectures he gave himself to knock it off, he fumed, his mind kept replaying the entire evening at Marsha and Bud's over and over. He saw the beautiful expression of pure love on Caitlin's face when she'd looked at her daughter's photographs, and remembered the tears that had glistened in both Marsha and Bud's eyes as they'd gazed at the picture of Grace.

What an unbelievable night it had been for the people in that room. Dreams were coming true for those who had waited so long to have them fulfilled. Incredible.

Matt sighed and slid both hands beneath his head. He had been included in everything that had happened this evening but...not quite. Circumstances dictated that he stand on the edge of the circle of sunshine those match pictures had created, congratulate the new parents, wish them well.

But none of those photographs declared him to be a daddy because that wasn't *his* dream, his heartfelt desire, and he hadn't completed the tons of paperwork and waited the seemingly endless months as the others had.

He was grateful to have witnessed such happiness, such joy, was very honored to know he was to be Grace's godfather, was pleased he would be helping Caitlin, the lovely Caitlin, put the finishing touches on the nursery that would be waiting for Mackenzie or Madison when she arrived in her new home.

But…yeah, so okay, he was willing to admit that there had been flickers of chilling emptiness that had consumed him earlier. He'd been so aware of his…his aloneness, of the narrow focus of his life, had been forced to wonder if perhaps, just maybe, he was not only alone but might also be lonely.

"Ah, hell, come on, MacAllister, knock it off," he said, pulling his hands from beneath his head and dragging them down his face. "That's nuts."

The structure of his existence was of his making, his choice. He was centered on a challenging and rewarding career at Mercy Hospital that gave him a great deal of satisfaction. Granted, it was a tad rough on his physical well-being, but he'd get a handle on that, take control of that aspect of it.

Sure, he wanted a family someday, a wife, kids, a home bursting at the seams with love and laughter. He'd take part in the whole program…change diapers, teach each munchkin in turn to ride a bike, mow the lawn, take out the trash, help with homework and housework and read stories to sleepy bundles tucked safely on his lap. Yeah, he wanted all of that, plus a wife he'd love beyond measure and who would love him in kind.

Someday…but not now.

Hell, he was only thirty-two years old. He had plenty of time to join the rank and file of the MacAllisters who toted diaper bags to family gatherings. Plenty of time.

What had happened tonight at the Mathises' house was perfectly understandable. He'd been caught up in the emotions of the people there. He'd felt a momentary sense of aloneness and…okay… loneliness simply because he was odd man out in what had been a rather unusual situation.

There. He'd figured it all out. It had just taken a bit of logical thinking to get his head on straight again. He could now go on the trip to China, enjoy the entire thing, spend time with the very lovely Caitlin Cunningham, then return home and shortly afterward return to the hospital and the career that gave him everything he needed in his life now.

His reputation for being one of the best publicrelations directors of a large hospital was rock solid across the country, and he had several awards framed and hanging on his office wall. The name Matt MacAllister meant something in his field and he would continue to maintain that level of expertise.

Matt rolled onto his stomach, closed his eyes, mentally patted himself on the back for his rather genius-level thinking that had solved the jumbled maze in his mind, then drifted off to sleep.

But through the night he dreamed of Caitlin. He was standing next to her in a room where they were surrounded by babies, each holding up little arms toward them, wanting to be held, comforted, loved. Wanting to be taken home.

Chapter Three

The next day was another long stretch of hours at the hospital as Matt once again dealt with Homer Holmes, the note-taking attorney. Matt finally glanced at his watch and inwardly cheered.

"Time to wrap it up, Homer," Matt said. "I have an important appointment to keep. In fact, we've covered everything that is pending. Starting tomorrow you're on your own."

"Listen, Matt," Homer said. "I've been admiring that miniature antique scale you have on the corner of your desk."

"The scale?" Matt said. "My grandfather gave that to me months ago. The workmanship is exquisite, don't you think? The chains holding the two small trays have the exact number of links, you can see the intricate scrollwork on the base...even the two gold coins in that one tray are antiques. It was a very special gift from a remarkable man, and I treasure it.''

''That's what I was getting at. It's obviously worth a great deal of money, and I'm afraid I might bump it, send it toppling to the floor, harm it in some way. Don't you think it would be a good idea to take it home during this time you'll be away from the hospital?''

Matt shrugged. ''I suppose I could but... No, I'll just move it to the bookshelves against the wall. I like to be able to see it, and this is where I spend the majority of my time.''

Matt picked up the scale, crossed the room and set it carefully on a shelf on the bookcase.

''There,'' he said. ''Feel better?''

''Much,'' Homer said, nodding. ''Is it a family heirloom?''

''No.'' Matt stared at the scale. ''My grandfather chose it especially for me. He selected special gifts for each of his grandchildren. I've heard the story behind some of the presents, the fact that our grandfather was delivering an important message to the recipient with the gift.

''In my case, there's no hidden message as far as I can figure out. It's just an extremely rare and terrific present.'' He looked at his watch again. ''I'm out of here. Take good care of my baby while I'm gone.''

''Your...what?''

''The hospital. It's where I direct all my energies, like a parent would toward a child and... Never mind. Bye.''

Matt strode from the room, leaving a rather bemused Homer behind.

Caitlin frowned at her reflection in the full-length mirror on the inside of her closet door.

Satisfied now? she asked herself. This was the third outfit she'd tried on. Well, she wasn't changing her clothes again. Jeans, tennis shoes and a peach-colored string sweater. That was it. Except...maybe the blue knit top would be better because...

''You are acting like an idiot, Caitlin Cunningham,'' she told her reflection, ''and I've had enough of this nonsense. This isn't a date, it's a mission, the purpose of which is to complete the nursery for your daughter.''

Caitlin spun around, snatched her purse off the double bed and left the bedroom. In the living room she placed her purse on an end table and sank onto the sofa.

Matt MacAllister, she fumed, had driven her crazy the entire day. Every time she looked at the match pictures she'd placed on the corner of her desk at work, the image of Matt inched its way into her mental vision.

In a way, that made sense. She needed to get the nursery ready.

Matt was going to make it possible for her to accomplish that, so when she gazed at the photographs of Miss M., it stood to reason that Matt would trek right in front of her mind's eye, too.

So, okay, it made sense…to a point. What didn't compute was why when she thought about Matt she got a funny flutter in her stomach and a sharp remembrance of Matt's strong-but-gentle arm encircling her shoulders last night. Thinking about that caused a strange heat to begin to swirl within her and… No doubt about it…Matt was driving her right over the edge.

Well, in all fairness to herself she was admittedly in the midst of an emotional upheaval because she was about to become a mother. After all these months, the hope, the dream, the prayer had finally come true. She was momentarily off kilter as she attempted to adjust to the wonderful, albeit a tad terrifying, news, and so she was overreacting to things she would normally just take in stride. Like Matt.

"Caitlin," she said aloud, "that was nothing short of brilliant the way you figured all that out. Thank goodness that mishmash is solved."

The doorbell rang and Caitlin jerked at the sudden noise, her heart racing as she hurried to the front door.

Matt stood on Caitlin's front porch and nodded in approval.

Nice place, he thought. Caitlin's home was small, as were the other houses on the block, but the neighborhood exhibited a great deal of pride of ownership. Caitlin's cottage…now, that had a nice ring to it…was painted country-blue with decorative white shutters edging the windows. The minuscule front yard was a lush carpet of green grass, plus a tall mulberry tree. When he'd pulled in to the driveway, he'd gotten a glimpse of a wooden fence enclosing the backyard. That was good. Miss M. would have a safe place to play. Well, so far, the outside of the house suited Caitlin. If she answered the door and let him in he'd get a glimpse of the inside.

Matt pressed the doorbell and a moment later Caitlin opened the door.

"Hi," Matt said. Oh, hey, what Ms. Cunningham did for a pair of snug jeans was something to behold.

Caitlin smiled as she stepped back to allow Matt to enter. "Come in, Matt." Matt MacAllister in jeans and a black knit shirt was causing that funny little flutter to slither down her spine again. Darn it. "How are you?" She closed the door.

"Fine." Matt swept his gaze over the living room. "Well, as fine as anyone could be after spending the day with an attorney who writes down everything, including what he had for lunch." He paused. "This is a very nice house, Caitlin. I like oak furniture myself and your colors are pretty…mint-green, and what would you call that? Salmon?"

Caitlin laughed. "I think I would call those colors a mistake for sticky toddler fingers. I didn't know when I made these selections that there would be a busy little girl living here. I'll worry about that later. Nothing can dim my excitement about becoming a mother."

"Good for you." Matt wandered across the room and looked at some of the titles of the books in a tall oak bookcase. "We have similar taste in authors, except I can't remember the last time I actually settled in and read a novel. There just aren't enough hours in the day."

"Perhaps you'll find the time while you're off work during this month or so Bud sentenced you to."

"Maybe, but I doubt it. I'll be in China for a couple of weeks, then when I get back I have a feeling I'll be on the phone more often than not with the guy who's taking my place for now. He doesn't exactly evoke a great deal of confidence in being able to handle what needs to be done. Man, when I think about the messes he could create while... Nope, erase that. I'm not supposed to think about it.''

''I imagine that's impossible for someone like you to do.''

Matt turned to look at her. ''Someone like me? Somehow that doesn't sound like a compliment.''

''I just meant that you're obviously focused on your job, dedicated to your career to the exclusion of just about anything, or anyone, else. To suddenly just shut off your mind and stop thinking about it would be extremely difficult, impossible, in fact.

''Putting thousands of miles between you and the hospital will help, but even so, I would guess that part of your thoughts will be at Mercy. You won't be totally there with all of us.''

Matt frowned. ''Is this the voice of experience I'm hearing? Have you been completely centered on your career in the past?''

''Me? Heavens no.'' Caitlin shook her head. ''I enjoy being a copywriter for the fashion magazine. It's very challenging and the work is continually fresh and new, but when I come home at night I don't think about it again until I report for duty the next day.''

''I see. The slight edge to your voice says you

don't approve of my 24/7 approach to my career, Caitlin."

"I'm sorry if I gave you that impression, Matt. It's certainly not my place to approve or disapprove of the way you conduct your life. Goodness, I don't even know you." She paused. "I think it would be best if we changed the subject. Even better, why don't we go have our pizza."

"Sure, we'll go for pizza, but let's change the subject first. Why did you decide to become a single mother?"

"Gosh, Matt, don't hold back, just ask me any personal question that pops into your head."

Matt chuckled. "I'm sorry. I guess it *is* rather personal, isn't it? But I'm interested in why you came to this decision. Not that you're obligated to tell me, of course."

"Let's just say that I believe this is the very best choice for me...personally. End of story. Subject closed. Shall we go?"

Matt nodded and followed Caitlin out the front door.

Oh, yes, he thought. The lovely lady did, indeed, have secrets that she didn't intend to share. So many questions surrounded Caitlin Cunningham, creating so many answers he intended to discover, one by one.

The pizza restaurant was popular and crowded, and Caitlin and Matt had a short wait before a booth became available. They decided on what toppings they wanted on their pizza and what they would drink, then Matt went to the counter to place their order.

"It'll be about fifteen minutes," he said, returning and sliding in across from Caitlin. "So. Have you made arrangements for day care for Miss M.?"

"I'm going to be working at home. I've already reached an agreement with my boss about it, and I've changed the third bedroom in the house into an office. Later, when Miss M. is ready to play with other children, I'll consider day care. Even if I had been matched with an older child, I planned to stay home with her at first because she'd have so many adjustments to make."

"Don't you think you'll get cabin fever working at home?"

"No, I don't believe so. I'll have my daughter with me, remember? Plus, she and I will be going back and forth to the magazine office to pick up and deliver work, connecting with other people. Once we get into a routine I should have a healthy balance during a given day."

"I hope it all goes the way you have it planned. Life has a way of throwing us curves when we least expect them at times. I'll keep my fingers crossed for you and Miss M. for smooth sailing ahead."

"That was a rather pessimistic statement." Caitlin frowned. "Life has a way of throwing us curves? Are you referring to yourself?"

"Me? No, no, not at all. My life is set up exactly the way I want it. I've hit a momentary glitch with this enforced-vacation bit, but things will get back to normal for me soon."

Caitlin nodded.

"The reason I said that about the throwing of curves," Matt went on, "is because I just saw a woman who reminded me of my cousin, Patty. She's going through a rough time right now and got more than her share of nasty curves, I'm afraid. I wasn't implying that anything would go wrong with your plans."

"Oh, I see." Caitlin paused, then looked directly at Matt. "You know, we seem to be just on the edge of getting into arguments no matter what topic we touch on tonight. There's a…I don't know…a tension between us that isn't very pleasant.

"If you'd rather not go shopping for baby supplies I'll certainly understand. We were all on such emotional highs last evening and… Anyway, we can have our pizza and forget about the other if you'd prefer."

Matt leaned forward and covered one of Caitlin's hands with one of his on the top of the table.

"No, Caitlin, I've been looking forward to this outing all day. I'm sorry if I've been short-tempered, or whatever. Hey, let's start over from right now.''

"I've been a bit brusque with you, too, and I apologize." She smiled. "All right. Hello, Matt, it's nice to see you again and I certainly thank you for your help with my grand endeavor this evening.''

"Hello, Caitlin," he said, not releasing her hand. "I'm glad to be of service.''

She had to get her hand back, Caitlin thought frantically. There was a tingling heat traveling up her arm and across her breasts, causing them to feel strangely achy as though needing a soothing touch. Now Matt was pinning her in place with his incredible brown eyes and her heart was beating like a bongo drum.

"That's our number," Matt said. "I'll be right back with a gourmet delight.''

Thank heaven for pizza restaurants that called out lifesaving numbers, Caitlin thought, drawing a steadying breath. Darn it, she had to get a grip on herself, stop this nonsense of being thrown so off kilter by Matt MacAllister's blatant masculinity. He touched her, she melted; he gazed at her, she dissolved. This would never do.

They were going to be together on a daily basis soon, and she couldn't fall apart every two seconds because Matt was close to her. Well, she'd probably be fine over there because she'd be focused on the baby. Her precious daughter.

Matt returned with a huge pizza and a pitcher of soda, then trekked back for plates, glasses and napkins.

''There,'' he said, sitting down. ''I think I have everything we need...except...'' He smiled at Caitlin.

''Except?'' she asked.

''You don't happen to have the pictures of Miss M. in your purse, do you? I sure would like to see that munchkin again. She's already stolen a chunk of my heart. I'm going to be putty in her tiny hands when I actually see her. Do you? Have the pictures?''

Oh, Matt just didn't play fair, Caitlin thought as unexpected and unwelcome tears stung her eyes. Why did he have to be so sweet, so endearing, on top of everything else he had going for him in the plus column. How many men would ask to see baby pictures as he was? Not fair at all.

Focus on the minus column, she told herself. This was Mr. I Work 24/7/365. He wouldn't be caught up in cute pictures of babies and putting cribs together if he weren't being forced to take a vacation. Matt was just filling idle hours with anything available. *Remember that, Caitlin. Don't you dare forget it.*

''Of course I have the pictures.'' Caitlin smiled.

''I never leave home without them. I took them to work today and Marsha and I drove everyone nuts poking our photographs under their noses.'' She handed the two pictures to Matt. ''Here she is.''

''Hey, kiddo. You're just as cute today as you were last night. That is wild hair. Maybe we should take her some of the goop, that styling-gel junk, that people use.''

We? Caitlin thought. *We* should take the baby some styling gel? Where had that *we* come from? Well, now, don't go crazy, Caitlin. Matt had been drafted into being her luggage handler or whatever his title was. Her partner, per se, because her friend couldn't go. So, it was natural that he'd see himself attached to her and the baby during the trip, in a manner of speaking.

Okay, she had that one figured out, but if she didn't quit analyzing and overreacting to everything that Matt said and did she was going to fall on her face from exhaustion. Food. She needed food.

''Food,'' she said, and reached for a slice of pizza.

Matt set the two pictures on the end of the table so both he and Caitlin could see them. They each ate a slice of pizza, and took a second one.

''This is delicious,'' Caitlin said.

''Mmm. You know, that one sleeper Miss M. has on looks okay, but the other one is really faded, worn. You can see how thin the material is in spots.''

"I know.'' Caitlin glanced over at the photographs. "The orphanages in China have to make due with what they can get. Miss M. is healthy, so that means she made it through the winter months after she was born without getting seriously ill. The weather in China now is much like it is here…warm, sunny. That makes me rest a little easier about the condition of that sleeper.''

Matt chuckled. "Maybe that's why she's frowning in both pictures. She's all girl and isn't satisfied with her wardrobe.''

"Oh, okay, I'll go with that theory, rather than one that says she's unhappy about something…like a tummyache or…oh, don't get me started. I'll worry myself into a sleepless night. I hope Carolyn calls soon and says we're scheduled to leave. I just want to go get my baby, my daughter. Marsha agrees with me that even though we've waited all these months, now that we've seen the pictures this is agony.''

"No joke. I wish she would have smiled in at least one of those photos. Nope. Whoa. We won't dwell on why she looks so grumpy.'' Matt narrowed his eyes. "New topic. Sort of. Have you settled on a middle name yet?''

Caitlin nodded, raised one finger as she chewed, then swallowed a bite of pizza. "Her middle name is going to be Olivia, after my mother. I not only love my mom but I also respect her more than I could ever begin to tell you. She conducted herself with such class and dignity through some very difficult years and, well, I thought that naming my daughter after her would really convey how I feel about her.''

''I think—'' Matt cleared his throat ''—I think that your mother must be very, very honored, Caitlin. I'd like to believe that I might have a daughter someday that thought that highly of me. What did your mother say when you told her?''

''She got all weepy, and Paulo, my stepfather, said it was a beautiful gift to give to her. My mother was a widow when she married Paulo last year. She met him during a trip she made to Italy, and it was a whirlwind courtship. Paulo is a delightful man who is crazy in love with my mother and they're so wonderful together. I'm thrilled for my mom. She deserves to have that kind of happiness.''

''You said your mother was a widow when she met Paulo.''

Caitlin nodded. ''Yes, my father died when I was sixteen.''

''Whew. That's rough. I'm sorry. Do you still miss him? Especially at a momentous time like this in your life when you're about to become a mother?''

"No. I don't miss him at all." There as a sudden sharp edge to her voice.

"Oh," Matt said, frowning slightly. Something wasn't quite on the mark here. There was a...a shadow hanging over the memory of Caitlin's father. Why? There he was again, stacking another question about Caitlin on the teetering tower. "You said last night that Paulo is ill?"

"Yes. They're running tests because they're not certain what is wrong and I'm very concerned about him. I'm praying he'll be fine and that he and my mother will be able to come to the States soon and meet Miss M."

"Who will be smiling by then," Matt said.

"Yes, she'll be smiling by then."

And then Caitlin and Matt were smiling as their gazes met, warm smiles, special smiles born of sharing the personal, meaningful story of why Caitlin had chosen the baby's middle name. The restaurant disappeared into a strange mist that surrounded them, the noise and the people simply no longer existed in the haze that swirled around them.

Their smiles faded as heat began to churn and thrum within them, pulsing, hot...so hot. They couldn't move, could hardly breathe, in the place they'd been transported to. It was so strange. And exciting. And terrifying. And...

"More to drink?" a voice said, snapping both

Caitlin and Matt back to reality with a thud. "It's all-you-can-drink night, refills free."

"It's who?" Matt said, staring at the young girl standing by their booth.

"Like...soda...ya know," the waitress said, pointing to the pitcher. "The drink? Free refills, like, twenty times if you want or whatever?"

"Oh. Sure." Matt nodded jerkily. "You bet. Fill it right up. Thank you. Nice of you to offer."

"Yeah, it's awesome," the girl said, snatching up the pitcher and eyeing Matt warily. "Back in a flash."

What had just happened between her and Matt? Caitlin wondered, fiddling with her napkin to avoid looking at him. She had never in her life experienced anything so...so unexplainable, so incredibly sensual and...

She wasn't going to address this. No. She'd just pretend that it hadn't happened. For all she knew, Matt hadn't even been aware of the strange... whatever it had been that had... It was over. Gone. Forgotten.

"So!" Caitlin said to a spot just above Matt's left shoulder. "Have you figured out how to pack enough for two weeks into one suitcase and..."

"Caitlin—"

"I've got to scrunch tons of diapers into my suitcase, along with baby clothes and bottles and... It certainly will be a challenge, that one suitcase, won't it? Yes, it definitely will and—''

''Caitlin—''

''What!'' she said much too loudly.

''I felt it. You felt it, I know you did. What… what was that?''

Caitlin plunked one elbow on the table and rested her forehead in her palm.

''I have no idea. And I don't care to discuss it, nor try to figure out what it was.''

''Why not?''

Caitlin raised her head. ''Why not? Because it was…was man-and-woman…stuff, and I don't want that in my life, complicating things. I am focused on mommy-and-baby…stuff, and that's all I can handle.

''I wish I could think of a more sophisticated word than *stuff,* but I'm a bit jangled at the moment. Whatever that was, Matt, it's in the past already, poof, gone.'' She lifted her chin. ''Please don't refer to it again.''

''You don't want me to refer to the fact that we're attracted to each other,'' Matt said, his gaze riveted on Caitlin. ''That there was suddenly such heated sexuality weaving back and forth between us that it's a wonder the pizza didn't burn to a crisp?

''You don't want me to tell you that during that strange moment out of time it took all the willpower I had not to come around this table, take you in my arms and kiss you until neither of us could breathe? Am I understanding you correctly?''

Caitlin opened her mouth to reply in the affirmative, only to discover she had no air in her lungs so she could speak. She nodded her head.

"I see. Well, I'll certainly respect your wishes on the above-mentioned subjects. But, Caitlin? That doesn't mean I won't be *thinking* about what just happened here. *Thinking* about what it would be like to kiss those very kissable lips of yours and—''

"Soda refill," the waitress said, plunking the pitcher onto the table.

"Oh, I am so glad to see you," Caitlin said to the young girl. "I'm just delighted that you're here…right now."

"Got it," the girl said slowly. "I don't mean to be, like, rude or anything, but you folks are borderline weird. Bye." She hurried away.

Matt laughed. "Borderline weird, is it?''

"At least she was more articulate than me saying *stuff*," Caitlin said, smiling. "Oh, this is silly. Let's just finish up so we can get ready for Miss M.'s arrival. I am one hundred percent into my mommy *stuff* and I intend to stay there, Mr. MacAllister.''

Chapter Four

The crib and changing table were white to match the other nursery furniture Caitlin had purchased. Matt insisted on buying Miss M. a crib mobile with brightly colored, puffy felt clowns that pranced around in a circle to the tune of "Rock-a-Bye, Baby."

They loaded the large boxes into Matt's SUV, then trekked back into the mall to select blankets, crib sheets, sleepers, several two-piece outfits and a pretty, red dress.

Carolyn had said that it was traditional for all the children being adopted to wear red on their last night in China, as it was the Chinese color for health, happiness and prosperity. Matt refused to leave the clothing department until he found a pair of white socks with red bows to go with the dress.

The next stop was for diapers, bibs, bottles, formula and a pacifier that Carolyn had said the babies would need on the airplane because of the cabin pressure.

In each department Caitlin showed the saleswoman the pictures of Miss M. for advice as to what size to buy.

"It's a bit difficult to tell how big she is," one saleswoman said, "because no one is holding her for reference. She looks small for six months, I think, but better to have the clothes and diapers a little big than too small. Oh, she is so cute. What proud new parents you must be."

"Well, we're not..." Carolyn started.

"Not coming down off our cloud number nine for a very long time," Matt finished for her.

"Good for you," the woman said. "Now, let's get you what you need."

"Why did you allow her to believe that we're married and the parents of this baby?" Caitlin whispered to Matt as they followed the woman.

Matt shrugged. "That's what she assumed and it was easier just to go with it."

"Oh," she said, nodding.

That made sense, Caitlin thought as she placed packages of diapers in the cart. Why get into a lengthy explanation about how Matt was helping because her friend got hurt and couldn't make the trip and…yes, it was simpler to let it go. She and Matt looked the same as Marsha and Bud must as they were doing the same type of shopping, as well as the other people in their group.

The new mommies and daddies. Daddies and mommies. Daddies. Parents-to-be who were soon going to complete their family with a wonderful little daughter. Mommy, Daddy and Baby and…

Stop it, Caitlin, she ordered herself. She was getting caught up in the charade that Matt had put in place. Her daughter was getting a loving mother.

"Baby wipes," Matt said, dropping a box into the cart. "Great invention."

"You sound like an expert on the subject," Caitlin observed, pulling her thoughts back to attention.

"Hey, I'm a MacAllister. I've changed my share of diapers over the years. The MacAllister clan is very big on babies."

Caitlin laughed. "I've never changed a diaper in my life. I'm assuming it's not all that difficult. It isn't, is it?"

"I wouldn't say that. There's a definite technique to it. If you get a wiggly kid you can be in big trouble if you don't get that diaper on really fast. There's a lot of dexterity involved, wrist action, too."

"Oh, cut it out." Caitlin laughed. "You're making it sound like a person needs an engineering degree to do this.''

''That would help, yes,'' Matt said solemnly, then burst into laughter in the next instant. ''I had you going there for a while, didn't I? You should have seen your face. No, Caitlin Cunningham, changing diapers is not tough. Now then, do you want to discuss methods of burping a baby?''

''Just hand me another package of those wipes.''

Oh, this was a fun outing, she thought, and Matt was fun and funny. She felt so happy, carefree, so incredibly glad she was who she was. Well, that stood to reason. She was the one who was about to become a mother. But the extra gift of laughter that was accompanying this shopping trip was thanks to Matt MacAllister. She'd remember this evening because it was very, very special.

Back at the house, Caitlin insisted on washing all the baby clothes while Matt was assembling the crib and changing table.

''Don't forget to wash the diapers, too,'' he said, peering in his toolbox.

''Wash the…Matt, those are disposable paper diapers.''

''See?'' He grinned at her. ''You know more about diapers than you thought you did. If you were a complete dunce about those nifty things you would have dumped them all in the washing machine. I'm just trying to boost your confidence, my dear.''

''You're cuckoo,'' Caitlin said, pointing one finger in the air.

''I know.'' Matt chuckled. ''But I'm loveable. Ah, here's the screwdriver I want.''

Lovable, Caitlin thought as she left the room with an armload of clothes and blankets. Lovable? As in, Matt was a man who would be easy to love, fall in love with? No, that last mental babble needed to be split in two.

Yes, Matt probably would a man who would be easy to fall in love with because he had it all at first glimpse—looks, charm, intelligence, a marvelous sense of humor, and on the list went.

But easy to love? To be a partner with, the other half of the whole? No. Matt the workaholic, the man so dedicated to his career that he had put his own health at risk, so focused on his position at Mercy Hospital to the exclusion of everything and everyone, would not be an easy man to be in love with.

It would, in fact, be impossible to be in a serious relationship with Matt because he wouldn't do his share, wouldn't help nurture the love. And like a flame of a candle struggling to stay warm and bright, that love would eventually be snuffed out, leaving the place where it had been in chilling darkness.

Caitlin frowned as she put the baby clothes in the washing machine, then held up the sweet little red dress before adding it to the load.

Where on earth, she thought, was all this heavy, nonsensical rambling coming from? She hardly knew Matt MacAllister. Yet she had jumped all the way from "How do you do, it's nice to meet you" to passing negative judgment on the man as a life partner. Ridiculous. Really dumb.

Caitlin added detergent to the wash, closed the lid on the machine, turned it on, then headed back to the nursery to see how the mechanic was coming along with the assembling of the crib for precious Miss M.

Matt finished his projects just as Caitlin was putting the last of the freshly washed purchases in the dresser.

"Done," he said.

"Me, too," she said, turning to smile at him. "Oh, this room looks perfect, Matt. Thank you so much."

"You're welcome," he said, then wound the mobile, causing the perky clowns to march in a circle as the music played. "Dynamite."

Caitlin laughed. "That mobile is so cute. It's a terrific gift for Miss M. and *she* thanks you, too. Now all we need is that telephone call from Carolyn saying it's time to pack our meager little suitcase and get ready to go. Oh, I get goose bumps just thinking about it.''

''Yep.'' Matt nodded. ''You know, I think 'Rock-a-Bye, Baby' is a waltz, of sorts. Ms. Cunningham, may I have this dance?''

''Are you serious?''

Matt closed the distance between them, drew Caitlin into his arms, then began to move her around the center of the room in time to the lilting music. Caitlin stiffened for a moment, then allowed Matt to nestle her close to his body.

And they danced.

They weren't in a huge ballroom dressed in their finery, with chandeliers twinkling above them as a band played. They were in a medium-size bedroom that had been transformed into a nursery decorated in yellow and white and that was waiting for a precious baby to arrive from the other side of the world.

They danced.

Not to the music produced by professional musicians in tuxedos, but to the tune accompanied by smiling clowns in brightly colored outfits who were keeping step to the music.

They danced.

It was a silly thing to do, yet it was the perfect thing to do, and Caitlin sighed in contentment as she savored the strength of Matt MacAllister, the aroma that was uniquely his, the feel of his tall, solid and nicely muscled body.

The music slowed, the clowns swung lazily around in their circle, then stopped as the last note played and a silence fell over the room.

The dance is over, Matt thought. He had to let Caitlin go and step away from her. But, oh, man, she felt fantastic in his arms, so delicate, so feminine, fitting against him as though custom-made just for him. She smelled like flowers and sunshine, and her dark curls had been woven from silken threads.

He had a feeling…oh, yeah, he knew…that he was going to remember this dance for a very, very long time.

Slowly and reluctantly, Matt eased Caitlin away from him, then dropped his arms to his sides. He nearly groaned aloud when he saw the dreamy expression on her face, the soft smile on her lips.

He wanted to kiss her, he thought. She was so beautiful, so womanly, and their dance had been so special and, damn it, he wanted to kiss her.

Don't do it, MacAllister, he ordered himself. Don't even think about it.

"Well," Matt said a tad too loudly. "I guess I'd better be on my way."

Caitlin blinked. "Oh. Yes, of course, I… Would you like a dish of ice cream?"

No, Matt thought. He was treading on dangerous

ground, his desire for Caitlin liable to be stronger than his common sense. He was going to leave right now, get a solid night's sleep and be back to normal in the morning. Yes, that was exactly what he was going to do.

"Ice cream sounds great," he heard himself say, then glanced around quickly with the irrational thought that he would discover the source of his reply.

"It's mint chocolate chip."

"Sold," Matt said. To the jerk who should be walking out the door. "That's one of my favorites."

Why had she done that? Caitlin asked herself as Matt followed her to the kitchen. Why hadn't she escorted Matt to the door, thanked him again for his help with the nursery, then closed the door on his gorgeous face before she did something else as ridiculous as dancing in the middle of a not-even-here-yet baby's room?

That would have been the smart thing to do. But, oh, no, not her. She was now about to share a sinfully delicious dessert with Matt and prolong this unsettling evening even more. Where was her brain?

Caitlin sighed as she removed a carton of ice cream from the freezer.

Her brain, she thought, plunking the carton on the counter, had gone south the moment Matt had taken her into his arms. Well, all she could do now was shovel in the ice cream as quickly as possible, plead fatigue, then...finally and overdue...send Matt on his way.

"I'll serve that up if you like," Matt said. "How many scoops do you want?"

"One." Caitlin set two bowls next to the carton. "Just one. Small. A small one. I'm going to go check my answering machine for messages while you do that. I'll be right back."

Matt watched as Caitlin nearly ran from the kitchen, then he turned to open the carton of ice cream.

Caitlin was jangled, he thought. It made him feel a tad better knowing that she had been just as affected by the dance as he had. It fell under misery loves company, or some such thing.

But if she was struggling with desire as he was, why had she invited him to stay for dessert? He didn't know the answer to that one. Caitlin was definitely not the type who was inching toward enticing him into her bed after they'd had their snack. Not even close. He knew that, just somehow knew that.

"Matt," Caitlin said, rushing back into the room. "Oh, you won't believe this. Well, maybe you will, but *I* can't." She stopped by his side and pressed her palms to her flushed cheeks. "Can you? Believe it?"

Matt chuckled. "I don't have a clue if I can, or can't, because I don't know what you're talking about."

"Oh. Yes." Caitlin patted her cheeks. "I'm going over the edge." She drew a quick breath. "Okay. I'm fine. There was a message from Carolyn on my machine. We're leaving Sunday morning for China. This is Thursday, Matt, and we leave on Sunday. Oh, my gosh. I can't believe this."

Matt replaced the carton of ice cream in the freezer, then carried the bowls to the table at the end of the kitchen.

"Come sit down and have some of this before you either faint, or float away on your happy cloud." He paused and frowned. "Sunday morning? Whew. I'm scheduled to make a couple of speeches, attend some fund-raising events and... Homer just isn't cut out for going in there cold. This is very short notice to find people to take my place."

Caitlin slid onto a chair at the table. "It's wonderful notice."

Matt settled on the chair opposite her and took a bite of ice cream.

"Mmm. Great stuff," he said. "Are you going to be able to sleep tonight? You're so excited you're about to bounce off the walls."

"I know." Caitlin smiled brightly. "I can't stop smiling. In just a handful of hours I'll be on an airplane winging my way toward Mackenzie or Madison.''

"Take a bite of ice cream. You're eating for two now.''

Caitlin laughed. "That's true, in a way. I *am* getting closer and closer to being a mother. Oh, Matt, we leave on Sunday.''

Matt reached across the table, covered one of Caitlin's hands with one of his, and smiled at her warmly.

"I'm sincerely happy for you, Caitlin,'' he said. "I really am. Your excitement, joy, is contagious, too. I'm certainly looking forward to seeing Miss M. for the first time, instead of just looking at her pictures. That is going to be quite a moment.'' He released her hand and picked up his spoon again. "I'd better polish this off. After all, I'm also eating for two.''

"Pardon me?'' Caitlin said, leaning toward him slightly.

Matt shrugged. "Well, think about it for a minute. I'm taking the place of your assistant, your girlfriend who flunked roller derby 101. So, for all practical purposes, as I take on the role she would have had during the length of the trip, I become Miss M.'s…surrogate father.''

Chapter Five

The hours until the group was to meet at the airport Sunday morning were filled with a flurry of activity for Caitlin.

Very early on Sunday morning Caitlin received a telephone call from Matt suggesting that he pick her up, as there was no point in both of them leaving their vehicles in long-term parking. To Caitlin's self-disgust she could not think of a reasonably reasonable reason why that wasn't a good idea and agreed to Matt's offer, reminding him that they'd have to put Miss M.'s car seat in his SUV.

When the group gathered at the designated gate at the airport, with everyone being much earlier than they needed to be, they were a very excited, emotional and exhausted bunch of people.

Elizabeth Kane, the director of the adoption agency, laughed when she saw them and said not to fear, because they were facing a fifteen-hour nonstop flight, which would give them plenty of time to catch up on their sleep. "And you'd better do just that," she said, beaming at them all, "because leisurely naps and undisturbed nights are soon to be a thing of the past."

"Oh, I know," one of the women said. "Isn't that wonderful?"

After what seemed like an endless wait, they boarded the plane, Matt having been assigned the seat next to Caitlin. Since Matt was to be Caitlin's extra pair of hands, Elizabeth explained, she thought by seating them together it would give them a chance to get to know each other better.

When the engines rumbled and lifted the huge aircraft off the ground, Caitlin closed her eyes.

"Are you afraid of flying?" Matt said, glancing over at her.

Caitlin opened her eyes and smiled at him.

"No, not at all. I'm just savoring the fact that we're on our way, actually on our way at long last." She paused. "Did you accomplish everything you needed to do at the hospital?"

Matt nodded. "It was down to the wire, but I did it. I haven't gotten more than a few hours' sleep in the last three nights, though. But as Elizabeth said, I can catch up during this flight. Fifteen hours. Man, that is grim. I plan to sleep, sleep, sleep during this trip. If I snore, just poke me.''

"I certainly will," Caitlin said, laughing.

Do not, Caitlin told herself, dwell on the image "poke me if I snore" evoked in her mind. Too late. She could feel the warm flush staining her cheeks.

During the flight the international dateline was crossed, and by the time the plane landed in Hong Kong in the early evening, no one was certain what day it was or how far off their physical clocks were.

They were transported to a nice hotel by a waiting van, checked in as a group by Elizabeth and arranged to meet again in the lobby in an hour to go out to dinner.

"We'll be going to a restaurant a few blocks from here," Elizabeth said, "so we can walk, and I've made a reservation, so they're expecting us. My groups always eat there during this stopover in Hong Kong.

"I took the liberty of ordering for all of us, and there will be a multitude of dishes on a lazy Susan in the center of the table. You'll have the opportunity to sample all kinds of delicious offerings."

On the third floor, where the entire group had been booked, Caitlin used a plastic key card to open the door to her room, settled her suitcase on the luggage rack, then snapped on a lamp. She frowned as the bulb remained dark. Moving carefully in the darkness she tried another lamp with the same result.

She inched her way back to the door and opened it to allow the lighted hallway to cast a dim glow over her room, then frowned.

She would, she supposed, have to find the telephone, wherever it was hiding in there, and call down to the desk to tell them the electricity wasn't working.

The door directly across from her opened suddenly and Matt appeared, his room brightly lit behind him.

"Problem?" he asked.

"I apparently don't have any electricity. None of the lamps work."

"Do you have your key card?"

"My...yes." Caitlin held up the card that was still in her hand.

Matt took it and slipped it into a slot on the wall by the door beneath the light switches. The lamps Caitlin had fiddled with immediately lit up.

"Let there be light."

"For goodness' sake. How did you know that was what to do?"

"I read the material the airline provided while

you were playing what must have been over a thousand games of gin rummy with the others.''

''Oh.''

''May I see what kind of view you have from your window?'' Matt asked. ''I'm staring at the rear of the building behind us.''

''Oh, well, sure, of course, go right ahead.''

As Matt crossed the room, the door closed and Caitlin stared at it for a long moment.

Dandy, she thought. Now she and Matt were together in her room with the door closed. What if the others saw them come out when it was time to meet in the lobby? She'd spent as much time as possible, when she wasn't sleeping on the airplane, playing cards and visiting with the others instead of sitting by Matt as though they were a couple. The last thing she wanted was for rumors to start about a possible romance between her and Matt MacAllister.

So far she hadn't been aware of any speculative glances or sly smiles directed their way, but exiting her room with Matt would not be a terrific idea. She was hoping that the group would continue to remember that Matt was simply stepping in to help her out.

She had no intention, Caitlin thought, of using up any mental or emotional energy that should be directed toward her daughter denying queries about what was taking place between her and Matt. Especially since nothing was taking place between her and Matt. Nothing at all.

So what if she'd been aware of how peaceful he appeared when he slept, yet still had that aura of blatant masculinity emanating from him?

So what if she thought it was so endearing the way he rubbed his eyes with his fists like a little boy when he first woke up?

So what if there was a rugged earthiness about him that sent shivers down her spine when he needed a shave?

None of that was important. It didn't mean a thing.

"Las Vegas," Matt said from over by the window. "That's what Hong Kong reminds me of. Lots of neon lights, people crowding the sidewalks, noise, cars, the whole nine yards. Come look at this, Caitlin. See if this view doesn't remind you of Las Vegas."

"I've never been to Las Vegas," she said, staying by the door.

"Oh, well, come take a look anyway."

With a silent sigh, Caitlin crossed the room and joined Matt at the window. He slipped one arm across her shoulders, then pointed toward the street below.

"See? You'd never know you were in an Asian country. That is due, madam, to the fact that Hong Kong was under British rule for many, many years before once again being claimed by mainland China, and is very westernized, if there is such a word. However, when we arrive in Nanjing tomorrow, then later go on to Guangzhou, you will experience the real China of today.''

''Do tell.'' Caitlin managed to produce a small smile.

Matt had nestled her close to his body, she thought frantically. His big, strong, oh-so-warm body. Such heat. It was weaving its way from him into her, swirling within her, then pulsing low and hot. He was being so nonchalant about having his arm around her, acting as though it didn't matter, just happened to be where it had landed. Well, she could match him sophistication for sophistication, by golly. Unless she fainted dead out on her face first.

''I *am* telling you,'' Matt said, chuckling, ''so pay attention, because people pay tour guides *beaucoup* bucks for information like this.''

''I'm etching it all on my weary brain. I even got a bonus because now I know what Las Vegas looks like back in the States.'' She cleared her throat. ''Well, thank you for solving the mystery of the electricity. You were a hero to the rescue of a damsel in the darkness.''

Matt turned his head to smile at her, but his smile disappeared quickly as he realized that Caitlin was only inches away. His gaze swept over her delicate features, lingered on her lips, then he looked directly into her dark eyes.

"I don't think," he said, his voice husky, "that I'd be off base if I kissed you, Caitlin. After all, we *have* slept together."

Caitlin blinked. "We…we what?"

"Slept together. On the plane. Right there, side by side, we both were sleeping. So, therefore, we slept together. Sort of."

"That's the silliest—"

"No," he interrupted, lowering his head slowly toward hers, "it's not. And there is nothing silly about how much I want to kiss you, how long I've waited to kiss you, or about the fact that I'm about to kiss you."

And he did.

Caitlin stiffened as Matt brushed his lips lightly over hers, then shivered when he repeated the sensuous journey. He encircled her with his arms and pulled her close to his rugged body as he intensified the kiss, parting her lips to slip his tongue into the sweet darkness of her mouth.

Caitlin's hands floated upward to entwine behind Matt's neck, then her lashes drifted down as she savored the taste, the feel, the aroma of Matt.

She'd fantasized about this kiss, she thought hazily, dreamed about it, had been waiting, as Matt had, for it to take place.

Nothing more should, nor would, take place between them, she silently vowed, but this kiss was theirs to share, the memories of it to do with as they each desired.

Matt lifted his head just enough to draw a quick, sharp breath, then his mouth captured Caitlin's once again in a searing kiss.

Oh, Matt, Caitlin thought as she trembled in his arms. He had picked the perfect place for this to happen. Hong Kong was…was sort of in limbo, a place of bright colors and surging crowds, a mixture of cultures, the old, the new, creating an otherworldly aura.

It wasn't the reality of Ventura, nor of the China where her daughter waited. What happened between her and Matt here in Hong Kong was separate and apart from what truly existed. So be it.

Matt broke the kiss, took a rough breath, then eased Caitlin gently away from his aroused body.

"I should apologize for doing that," he said, his voice gritty with passion, "but I can't because I'm not sorry. I've wanted to kiss you from the moment I saw you, Caitlin. Before you decide to be mad as hell, remember that you shared these kisses, held nothing back."

"I'm not angry," she said, her voice unsteady. "I wanted that to happen as much as you did, Matt. The sensual tension between us has been building and building and… But that's over, now, done.

Nothing like this is going to take place between us again.''

Matt frowned and dragged a restless hand through his hair.

''I don't understand. We just shared kisses that were sensational, unbelievable. We also get along great together, have fun, laugh, talk. Something is going on here, Caitlin. Don't you want to know what it is?''

She took a step backward and wrapped her hands around her elbows. ''No, Matt, I don't.''

''Why in the hell not?'' he said none too quietly.

''Because,'' she said, dropping her hands to her hips and matching his volume, ''I am on this trip for one purpose. One. My daughter. She is all I'm focusing on. I certainly don't intend to fit a short-term affair in around the edges of my busy schedule over here. No, I'm not sorry about the kisses, but nothing else is going to... No.''

''You're making whatever this is between us sound cheap and tacky, Caitlin. I resent that.''

''Well, excuse me to hell and back,'' Caitlin said, plunking down on the edge of the bed. ''Okay, you don't like my short-term-affair description. Fine. What would you call it if we continue, end up in bed together?

''Tell me, Matt. Have you been struck by Cupid's arrow, fallen head over heels in love with me, intend to not rest until I agree to marry you?''

"Oh. Well, no, but give me a break here. That sort of stuff only happens in the movies or those romance novels that women read. Let's be realistic."

"I am being realistic. We're sexually attracted to each other, plus we have fun together, enjoy each other's company. However, since we're not in love with each other, taking this further would be nothing more than a short-term affair. I rest my case."

"I have never in my life," Matt said, a rather bemused expression on his face, "had a conversation like this one with a woman. Talk about analyzing something to death. I mean, I'm used to just letting things take their natural course and…then…later, down the road it's…" His voice trailed off.

"Aha." Caitlin pointed one finger in the air. "Down the road it's over, ending yet another short-term affair of which I speak."

"Would you cut that out?"

Before Caitlin could reply, a knock sounded at the door.

"Caitlin," came Marsha's muffled voice. "Are you ready to go down to meet the others for dinner? Caitlin?"

"Oh, good grief." Caitlin jumped to her feet. "That's Marsha."

Matt grinned. "Shall I get the door while you freshen your lipstick?"

"Don't you touch that door," Caitlin whispered. "Marsha's busy little mind will go nuts if she finds us in here together."

"Caitlin?" Marsha called. "Are you in there?"

"Yes, I'm here," Caitlin yelled. "Go on ahead, Marsha. I'll be along in just a couple of minutes."

"Okay. Have you seen Matt? He isn't in his room."

"Oh, he's around somewhere. Maybe he already went downstairs."

"Well, hurry up, because I am starving to death."

"I will. I just have to comb my hair."

"And freshen your lipstick," Matt said with a chuckle, which earned him a glare from Caitlin.

Caitlin ignored Matt to the best of her ability as she freshened up.

Matt folded his arms loosely over his chest and leaned one shoulder against the wall as he waited. Oh, Caitlin was something, he thought. The kisses they'd shared had been sensational. She was very sensual, very womanly and obviously was comfortable with her own femininity. She had returned his kisses in total abandon and he had been instantly aroused, wanting her, aching for her with an intensity like nothing he'd known before.

And Caitlin when angry? Dynamite. Her cheeks

became flushed and her eyes flashed like laser beams. She'd taken him on, toe to toe, and let him know what he could do with any ideas that he might be entertaining of a short-term affair with her.

Matt frowned.

Short-term affair. Caitlin had repeated that phrase like a broken record until he'd reached the point that he'd told her to put a cork in it. The problem was, she was right. He had nothing more than the now ever-famous short-term affair to offer her. He simply wasn't ready for a commitment to forever, a relationship that would inch toward marriage, hearth, home and Miss M. the baby.

Yeah, sure, he'd said he'd like to know what was happening between Caitlin and him because it was definitely…different somehow from his past experiences where casual dating was the order of the day and no one got hurt. No, there was more depth, intensity between him and Caitlin. But that didn't mean he was opening the door to a possible permanent future with her and the daughter she would see and hold for the first time tomorrow.

So, where did that leave him? Aching for Caitlin. Wanting to make love with her. Envisioning pulling her into his arms and kissing her senseless at every opportunity, which would no doubt result in her popping him right in the chops.

''Well, hell,'' Matt said under his breath.

He had volunteered to stick like glue to Caitlin to be ready to assist her in any way he was needed. He was the extra pair of hands, hands that would not be allowed to touch her again. This trip was suddenly losing its appeal. Big-time.

"I'm ready," Caitlin said, bringing Matt from his now-gloomy thoughts. "I'll go first, then you take the elevator after me. That way we won't arrive in the lobby at the same time and create a scenario ripe for rumor."

"Ripe for rumor?" Matt said with a burst of laughter. "I can sure tell you write for a living. You certainly have a unique way with words."

He paused and became serious. "Caitlin, I think you're making far too much of this business of us being seen together. Everyone is focused on their baby, that little munchkin waiting for them to arrive tomorrow. The last thing on the minds of anyone in our group is whether or not you and I are getting it on or... Well, I could have said that nicer, but you get the drift."

Caitlin opened her mouth to deliver a retort to Matt's statement, then frowned and snapped it closed again. A long, silent minute passed as she stared into space, deep in thought.

"You're right," she said finally, looking at Matt again. "I'm acting like an idiot. It's very self-centered of me to think that everyone would be in a twitter over what may, or may not, be going on between the two of us. I should be thinking about my daughter, too, not about how I felt when you kissed me, or how much I had wanted you to kiss me, or how long it seemed that I had been anticipating your kissing me, or…''

Caitlin's eyes widened and a flush stained her cheeks.

''I didn't just say all that,'' she said, shaking her head. ''Oh, tell me I didn't say all that. This is so embarrassing and… No, this is jet lag. Yes, that's what's wrong with me. I'm suffering from a severe case of jet lag. Food. Maybe food will help.''

Caitlin hurried to the door and flung it open.

''Let's go,'' she said. ''We're probably holding up the whole group. I need nourishment so my brain can start functioning like something I recognize again. Where's my key card?''

''It's still in the slot to turn on the electricity,'' Matt said, crossing the room slowly.

''I knew that,'' Caitlin said, pulling the plastic card free.

''You're sure we should ride down in the elevator together?'' Matt said, pulling the door closed behind them. ''I'll do whatever makes you comfortable.''

''Of course we'll go together,'' Caitlin said as they reached the elevator. ''You were the one who made me realize how silly I was being about all of this.''

"Mmm." Matt nodded. "Well, for the record, Caitlin, I felt as though I'd waited an eternity to kiss you, too, and I'm going to remember those kisses we shared. Oh, yes, ma'am, I certainly am."

As the elevator door swished open, Caitlin said, "The subject is closed."

"Hold the elevator," a man called as Caitlin and Matt stepped inside.

Matt pressed the proper button to keep the doors open, and another couple from the group hurried inside.

"Oh, I was so sure we'd kept the whole bunch waiting for us," the woman said, "but you're just going down, too. That makes me feel better. We wasted so much time trying to figure out how to get the electricity to work in the room."

"Really?" Matt said. "I read all about it on the plane."

"I was totally baffled," Caitlin said, "if that makes you feel better. I just stood there like an idiot wondering where the phone was so I could call for help. Matt came across the hall and poked the card in the little slot."

"Came across…" The woman paused. "Oh, that's right. You're not a couple, per se. It's so difficult to keep so many new people straight at the same time. You sat together on the plane and—"

"Honey," her husband said, smiling, "you wouldn't keep it straight if you had a scorecard to look at, because you are thinking about the baby, and everything else is just sort of floating on by you.''

Matt looked at Caitlin with a very smug expression. She rolled her eyes heavenward.

The addition of Caitlin, Matt and the couple with them on the elevator completed the group waiting in the lobby to go to dinner, except for a missing Elizabeth Kane.

Despite their jet lag everyone was in fine spirits and the chatter was lively and quite loud.

Marsha and Bud joined Caitlin and Matt and the four agreed they were looking forward to a meal that was not airplane food. Marsha reached up and swiped her thumb over the left edge of Matt's top lip.

''You should have freshened your lipstick before you came down here,'' she said, laughing merrily. ''I just removed the last dab. I mean, hey, either wear it or don't, whatever floats your boat.''

To Caitlin's amazement and delight, an embarrassed flush crept up Matt's neck and onto his face.

''Marsha,'' Bud said, chuckling, ''give Matt and Caitlin a break, would you? It's none of our business if they... Well, it's just none of our business.''

''Of course it isn't,'' Marsha said. ''But that doesn't mean I can just cancel being snoopy.''

''Changing the subject now,'' Bud said. ''I wonder what's keeping Elizabeth?''

As though she'd heard her name being called, Elizabeth emerged as the elevator doors swished open, and hurried across the lobby to join the others, glancing at her watch when she finally stopped.

"Only ten minutes late," she said, "but I'll still apologize for keeping you waiting. I was making my usual telephone call to Dr. Yang in Nanjing to confirm our plans. He'll notify the director of the orphanage that we're on schedule and good to go. Dr. Yang will leave a message for me at our hotel in Nanjing informing me of the time the vans will arrive to take us to the orphanage so you can meet your daughters.

"As you've been told, you'll have about an hour's visit with them tomorrow, then take them with you the next day when we go back to the orphanage to get them." She paused and laughed. "Uh-oh, there's no tissue box to pass around and some of you are getting weepy. Let's head for the restaurant before we flood this lobby."

Darkness had fallen and more neon lights had come alive when the group left the hotel and began the walk to the restaurant. The name Las Vegas was heard several times from the various conversations taking place.

Caitlin replayed in her mind the moment when Marsha had wiped the lipstick from Matt's lips and couldn't curb her smile. She should be totally mortified, she thought, but she wasn't. Matt had been so endearingly embarrassed, she'd wanted to give him a hug and tell him not to worry about what anyone might be thinking about the telltale clue, and to remember that he was the one who had said that new daughters were the main focus of the entire group, not the doings of Caitlin Cunningham and Matt MacAllister.

Elizabeth was greeted warmly when they arrived at the restaurant, and they were soon settled at a large round table with a lazy Susan in the middle.

Three waitresses appeared and began to place steaming hot, intriguing-appearing offerings of food on the turntable. Plates were soon piled high with the fragrant food, and they dug in.

"Did Dr. Yang say anything about the babies, Elizabeth?" one of the women asked. "Anything at all?"

"Only that they would be ready and waiting for you to see and hold them," she said, smiling.

"Oh-h-h," the woman said. "I can hardly wait. I hope the hours between now and then pass quickly. This is torture." She smiled at her husband. "Just think, Bill. Tomorrow we meet Emma Lin. Tomorrow."

"Yep," he said, matching her smile. "In the meantime, eat your dinner."

"Tomorrow," Caitlin whispered, staring into space.

Excited chatter erupted around the table centered

on the wondrous event that would take place the next day. Matt leaned close to Caitlin so only she could hear him.

"Tomorrow," he said, smiling at her when she met his gaze. "You'll meet your daughter. You'll hold her, look into her pretty eyes and know if she's Mackenzie or Madison. It will be one of those life-changing memories that will be etched in your mind forever."

"Yes," Caitlin said softly.

"And you know something, Caitlin? When I realize that I'll be right there to witness it all, I can honestly say there's no place else on this earth I'd rather be."

Chapter Six

Caitlin sat next to one of the windows on the rickety bus that had picked up the group at the Nanjing airport, her gaze riveted on the bustling crowds within her view.

Nanjing, she decided, was absolutely enchanting, an intriguing blend of the old and the new. There were tall, modern buildings next to small, shanty-type houses, and the number of people riding bicycles in the surging traffic seemed to outnumber those in automobiles.

Some of the people were dressed in clothes she might see in Ventura, while others were wearing traditional dark pants and boxy jackets that she'd seen so often in photographs of the Chinese populace. The weather was perfect, warm with a cooling breeze.

"Oh," Caitlin gasped as she witnessed yet another near miss of a car colliding with a bicycle. "It's dangerous out there. The people on those bikes are demanding equal space on the roads. Scary."

Matt leaned forward to look out the window, then immediately settled back again in his seat with a chuckle.

"I don't think watching that madness is good for my blood pressure. This makes driving in Los Angeles or New York City a leisurely outing. Whew."

"There are amazingly few accidents," Elizabeth said, overhearing what Caitlin and Matt were talking about. "It looks awful, but it's organized chaos, or some such thing. The majority of people can't afford cars, so the mode of transportation is most often a bike. There is a stiffer penalty for stealing a bicycle than a vehicle."

"Fascinating," Matt said, nodding.

"Caitlin," Marsha said from across the aisle, "you should be taking notes on some of this. I think with your talent for writing you could do some very interesting articles for the magazine from a fashion angle, make our readers feel as though they've actually visited China. It would be a nice way to add to your income while you're working at home, too.''

"In between changing Miss M.'s diapers." Matt chuckled.

"Babies do take naps, you know." Marsha frowned. "But I guess that's when you take one, too, or maybe get caught up on the laundry and what have you. I don't have a clue."

"We'll find out very soon, sweetheart," Bud said. "You know, I have to admit I'm getting nervous about meeting Grace for the first time. What if I scare the socks off her? She's almost a year old, so I imagine she has definite opinions about things...like her father is terrifying."

Marsha patted Bud's knee. "We'll just take it as it comes, give her space, time to get used to us. When we bring her back to the hotel tomorrow we'll let her call the shots. If she doesn't want us to hold her, we won't push it." She paused. "Oh, dear, now *I'm* getting nervous."

Elizabeth laughed. "Just relax. If your new daughters sense that you're uptight they'll react accordingly. My years of making these trips allows me to say with confidence that you'll all be pleasantly surprised at how quickly your girls adjust to you and their new environment. They're extremely resilient little ladies."

"Goodness," Caitlin said. "I never gave a thought to the idea that Miss M. might not...well, like me right off the bat. We've all fallen in love with our daughters by just looking at their pictures but...oh dear.''

''Don't get tense,'' Matt said. ''Miss M. will take one look at you and it will be love at first sight, Caitlin, you'll see. I don't believe in that stuff when it comes to adults, but babies? They know when they're connected to someone special. Everything will be just fine.''

As conversations started throughout the bus about what they were seeing out the windows, Caitlin cocked her head to one side and studied Matt, who looked at her questioningly.

''What?'' he said.

''You believe that babies are capable of experiencing love at first sight, but adults aren't?'' Caitlin asked. ''At what point in their lives do they change their view on the subject?''

''Well...'' Matt shrugged. ''I don't know. When we grow up and get worldly and wise, I suppose. Love at first sight? Give me a break. Love...adult, man-and-woman love...is something that grows over time, has to be nurtured, tended to, sort of like a garden that eventually produces beautiful flowers and... Jeez, I'm getting corny here.''

''No, you're not,'' Caitlin said quietly, looking directly into Matt's eyes. ''I think you expressed that very nicely, and I agree with you.''

''Which is why,'' Matt observed, switching his

gaze to the scene beyond the window, ''I don't see falling in love in my near future because I don't have time for the nurturing, doing my part in tending to the…well, to the garden.''

''I know,'' Caitlin said, then stared out the window again.

Well, Matt thought, he covered that topic very thoroughly, right on the mark. And for some unexplainable reason it had caused his ulcer to start burning with a hot pain as though voicing displeasure at what he had said.

Matt reached in his pocket, retrieved an antacid tablet and popped it into his mouth, frowning as he chewed the chalky circle.

''I saw that, MacAllister,'' Bud said. ''Whatever you're talking about over there, change the subject. Your doctor has spoken.''

''Cork it, Mathis.'' Matt glared at Bud.

The bus driver made a sudden sharp turn, and moments later they rattled to a stop in the circular driveway in front of a modern high-rise hotel.

''We have arrived,'' Elizabeth said. ''This is a lovely hotel, and you'll be very comfortable here. I'll check us in as a group again and hand out the key cards. It would be best if you'd wait in the lobby, though, while I telephone Dr. Yang and find out what time the vans are coming to take us to the orphanage. That will save me having to call each of your rooms to let you know. Okay?''

Elizabeth received quick, affirmative and excited answers to her request. The group was soon standing in the spacious, nicely furnished lobby with luggage at their feet and key cards in their hands as they waited to hear the outcome of her call.

They were all booked into the fourth floor, Elizabeth explaining that it kept crying babies from disturbing other guests. Matt glanced at Caitlin's key card, then his own, and nodded in approval that they were in side-by-side rooms.

Good, he thought. He'd be close at hand if Caitlin needed help with Miss M. She didn't have any experience with babies, while he had years of it due to being a MacAllister.

A MacAllister. Ah, yes, the powerful and well-known family of Ventura, the movers and shakers, the overachievers, who seemed to excel in whatever career choices they made. As each new generation came along, the pattern was repeated. Pick a subject? There was a MacAllister who did it…extremely well. Lawyers, doctors, architects, police officers, the list was endless. If you were a MacAllister, by damn, you'd better be top-notch at whatever you did or…

Whoa. Halt. Enough, he thought, frowning. Where was all this coming from? He was standing in a hotel lobby halfway around the world from Ventura and his clan. Why was he suddenly focusing on something that had hovered over him from the time he was a kid? A kid who wasn't good at sports in school, who had been an average student not a super brain, a kid who looked at the MacAllisters surrounding him and continually wondered why he fell short time after time after...

"Matt?" Caitlin said.

"What?" he said, looking at her.

"Do you have a headache? You're frowning and rubbing your forehead. Are you okay?"

"Oh, sure, sure, I'm fine." He forced a smile. "Just suffering from a bit of jet lag like everyone else." He paused. "Maybe I should figure out the time difference between here and Ventura and decide when I can call the hospital and see if everything is running smoothly."

Caitlin sighed. "I wondered how long it would take before you felt the need to do that. You're not focused on a new daughter like the rest of us. You're centered on your work."

"That's not true. I'm really eager to see Miss M., Caitlin, I told you that. Remember? I said there was nowhere else I'd rather be than—"

"Calling the hospital in Ventura," she interrupted, lifting her chin and meeting his gaze.

"Forget the call. I'm not going to do it. I'm not telephoning the hospital and checking up on things."

"Right." Caitlin rolled her eyes.

"I mean it. Cross my heart and hope to die, stick

a needle in my eye. Oh, hey, here comes Elizabeth.''

No one spoke as Elizabeth rejoined the group.

''Okay, we're on target,'' she said. ''It's four o'clock. Go unpack and be back down here at five ready to go to the orphanage.''

''Oh,'' Caitlin whispered. ''Oh, my goodness.''

Three new mommies-to-be burst into tears.

''Shoo, shoo,'' Elizabeth said, laughing and flapping her hands at them. ''Go to your rooms. There. I sound like a stern old auntie. I'll see you all back down here in an hour.''

Everyone collected their luggage, and Caitlin and Matt headed to their rooms.

Matt stopped as Caitlin poked the key card in the slot when they reached her room, then opened the door when the green light blinked on. She stepped inside the room far enough to hold the door open with her bottom and look back at Matt.

''I see the gizmo on the wall for the card so I can turn on the lights,'' she said, laughing. ''I'm a quick study.''

''Good for you, but maybe you should turn around and see what they've put in your room.''

Caitlin frowned slightly in confusion, turned, then a gasp escaped from her lips.

''Oh. Oh, Matt, look. It's a crib. A port-a-crib. It's Miss M.'s crib where she'll sleep after I bring her back here tomorrow. Isn't that the most beautiful thing you've ever seen?''

Matt's gaze was riveted on Caitlin as he heard the awe, the wonder, the heartfelt emotion ringing in her voice.

''Yes, I'm looking at one of the most beautiful things I've seen.'' He cleared his throat as he heard the rasp of building emotions in his voice. ''I'll knock on your door when it's time to go back downstairs. Okay?''

'''Kay,'' Caitlin said absently, starting toward the crib.

The door swung free and closed in Matt's face with a thud. He stood statue still for a long moment, attempting to visualize Caitlin inside the room, maybe running her hand over the rail of the crib, or across the soft sheet on the tiny mattress, or perhaps just gazing into the crib and envisioning Miss M. sleeping peacefully there, where she belonged, with her mother watching over her.

He looked quickly in both directions to be certain that no one had seen him standing there like an idiot who was attempting to carry on a conversation with a closed door before trudging back to his room.

Everyone in the group was fifteen minutes early arriving in the lobby, but no one settled onto the comfortable-looking chairs and sofas, not having the patience to sit still.

"What time is it?" Marsha said to Bud.

"One minute later than when you last asked me," he said, smiling. "Chill, pretty wife, or you're going to pass out cold on your nose."

"Oh, right," Marsha said, frowning at him. "Like you're Mr. Cool, huh? Might I mention that you forgot to tie your shoelaces?"

"Well, cripe," Bud said, looking down at his feet.

Matt whopped Bud on the back as he bent over to tend to his laces.

"Little shook up, Daddy?" Matt said. "Mmm. Maybe we should check your blood pressure, Doctor. You're in a high-stress mode."

"Can it, MacAllister," Bud said, straightening and glaring at Matt. "Caitlin, do something about this man."

"Me? What man?" she said, laughing. "I'm such a wreck I'm having trouble remembering my own name."

"The vans are here," a woman said, more in the form of a squeal.

"So they are," Elizabeth agreed, joining the group. "Is everyone ready? Let me count noses." She did a quick perusal of the gathered people. "Right on the money. Let's go meet some new baby daughters."

The fifteen-minute ride to the orphanage was a total blur to Caitlin until they suddenly turned onto a narrow street lined with small, shabby houses made of a variety of nonmatching material. At the end of the street a tall, seven-story building could be partially seen.

"That's the orphanage," Elizabeth said. "It's big, as you can see, and filled to the brim with kids. There are infant floors, where the little ones sleep two and three to a crib at times, toddler floors, then older children have several floors where they sleep dorm-fashion until they are fostered out to work in the fields in rural areas.

"There is no heat in that building. They have to layer the kids in lots of clothes in the winter to keep them warm. A portion of the fees you paid for this trip will go directly to the orphanage for food, clothes, medical supplies, what have you.

"The vast majority of the children are girls, as you know. The few boys that are brought here have some kind of medical problem, or perhaps a birthmark that is too noticeable, or they might have been the second boy in the family, breaking the law about only being allowed to have one child, and there isn't a thing wrong with them. However, it's rare for boys to be in the orphanages.

"And," Elizabeth said as the vans drove around a circle driveway. "Here—" the vans stopped "—we are."

Matt reached over and squeezed one of Caitlin's hands, finding it ice cold.

"Calm down," he whispered to her. "If you touch Miss M. with hands that cold she'll have a screamer of a fit."

Caitlin nodded jerkily.

A beaming Dr. Yang greeted the group as they entered the building. He was a slightly built man in his mid-thirties with handsome features and dark, almond-shaped eyes that seemed to be actually sparkling.

"I feel as though I know you," he said, his English having only a trace of an accent, "because I've read all of your dossiers. Welcome to China. Welcome to Nanjing. Welcome to the humble place where your daughters are waiting to meet you. Our elevator is very small, so I'll ask that you go up to the third floor four at a time, please.

"We will go into a living room, then I'll tell the head of the orphanage that you are here and that the caregivers should bring the babies to where you are. My paperwork is upstairs that documents the matches." He laughed. "Same as always, Elizabeth. You bring me people who are too nervous to speak."

"Never fails," she said, smiling.

"But soon they'll be crying those happy tears we always see," Dr. Yang said.

"They've been practicing those already. Okay, folksies. Here we go."

The living room Dr. Yang had spoken of was quite large, but the furniture and carpeting was very faded and worn. The paint on the walls was a color somewhere between gray and yellow and was peeling in numerous spots. There was a dusty, plastic red rose in a bud vase on a shabby end table in one corner. No pictures adorned the walls.

Caitlin, Matt, Marsha and Bud settled onto a threadbare sofa. Bud wrapped his arm around Marsha's shoulders and she sat as close as possible to him. Matt fought the urge to do the same to Caitlin as she sat next to him, her hands clutched so tightly in her lap the knuckles were turning white.

Elizabeth and Dr. Yang left the room and a heavy silence fell as the minutes ticked slowly by. Then everyone stiffened as the pair reappeared followed by caregivers in white uniforms, some holding one baby, others with two.

Dr. Yang consulted a sheet of paper he was holding, then placed his hand on the shoulder of one of the caregivers.

"Sally and Fred Roberts," he said.

And so it began, the uniting of parents and their daughters, with happy tears flowing freely. Marsha and Ben were called and their Grace gurgled and smiled when Marsha lifted her from the caregiver's arms and held her close, laughing and crying at the same time.

"That's my goddaughter. Awesome. You have to be next," Matt whispered to Caitlin, "because you're the only one left. Are you ready?"

"Oh, I am so ready," Caitlin said, staring at the empty doorway. "Why isn't there another caregiver standing there. Where's Miss M.? I don't understand why—oh…my…God. Matt, look."

Matt's eyes widened as a caregiver stepped into the living room, a baby tucked in the crook of each arm. Without realizing he was doing it, he grabbed Caitlin's hand and got to his feet, drawing her up next to him.

"Caitlin Cunningham," Dr. Yang said, smiling. "Last, but certainly not least."

"I…" Caitlin said, making no attempt to free her hand from Matt's as she walked toward the caregiver on trembling legs. "There are two… The pictures I got of Miss M. were of two babies, not just two photographs of the same baby. Dear heaven, they're identical twins. Twins? I'm going to be the mother of twins? Did I know this? I didn't know this. Oh, they're so beautiful, so… Twins?"

Dr. Yang frowned and looked at the sheet of paper. "Yes, it says here that you have been matched with identical twin girls of six months of age. Is there a problem?"

"Let's just all stay calm," Elizabeth said

quickly. "Caitlin, you and Matt take the babies to the sofa while I speak with Dr. Yang and see what is going on here. Dr. Yang, we at the agency and, therefore, Caitlin, didn't realize she'd been matched with twins. Nothing came across my desk indicating that."

"Really?" Dr. Yang said. "Well, come with me, Elizabeth, and we'll telephone Beijing, where all these decisions are made and discover what is taking place. Our caregivers have so much to do so…Caitlin? Matt, is it? Would you please tend to the babies until we return?"

"Yes, oh, yes," Caitlin said, lifting one of the infants from the caregiver's arms. "Matt?"

"Sure thing," he said, accepting the other baby. "Hello, Miss M." He glanced at the baby that Caitlin held. "Hello, Miss M. Man, they are really identical, aren't they? And they're both scowling, just like in the pictures you got. Let's go sit down and see if we can get them to smile. Caitlin?"

"Twins," she said, staring at the baby she held. "That's two. One plus one equals two. Twins."

"Sitting down now," Matt said, shifting the baby to one arm and gripping Caitlin's elbow. "Right now."

On the sofa, both Caitlin and Matt propped the babies on their knees, having to support their backs as they obviously were unable to sit up alone. Tears filled Caitlin's eyes as her gaze darted back and forth between the little girls.

"Oh, my gosh, they are so fantastic, so incredibly beautiful, and wonderful and…"

"And twins," Marsha said. "Caitlin, what are you going to do? You're a single mother, for Pete's sake. I'm scared to death about tending to Grace with Bud's help and you'll be all alone with two?" She paused and smiled. "But, oh, they are so cute. Grace, look at your little friends."

"Twin friends," Bud said. "Holy cow."

Matt bounced the baby a bit on his knees, then made a clucking noise that sounded rather like a sick chicken. The baby stared at him for a long moment, then a smile broke across her face, revealing two little teeth on the bottom gums.

"She smiled at me," Matt said, beaming. "Caitlin, look at Miss M. She's smiling."

Caitlin sniffled. "My Miss M. isn't smiling. I think she's about to cry."

"No way," Matt said, leaning toward the other baby and making the same ridiculous noise. The baby grinned, and she had the same two teeth on the bottom. "There you go. We've been waiting for that smile ever since we saw the pictures of her looking so grumpy. Well, actually it was the pictures of both of them looking so grumpy, but…" He shrugged. "Now they're smiling."

"They're so beautiful," Caitlin said, unable to

halt her tears. "I can hardly believe I'm actually holding… Oh, but, Matt, Marsha's right. How can I possibly cope, tend to, care for, twins? But they're my daughters. I fell in love with the baby in the photograph. So, okay, I didn't know I was falling in love with two babies but… Oh, dear, my mind is mush."

Dr. Yang and Elizabeth returned and came to where Caitlin and Matt were sitting.

"Um…Caitlin?" Elizabeth said. "Dr. Yang has something he wants to say to you. Hear him out, please, and don't…don't overreact to what he says. You must remember this is a culture far different from ours."

"Yes, well, we spoke to the person we needed to in Beijing. It seems a new employee in the office checked the wrong box on the final approval sheet, indicating you wanted twins. So, the match was made.

"The officials in Beijing said you are certainly cleared to take both of the babies if you so choose, but if not…" He shrugged and smiled. "Well, that's fine, too. It was a clerical error on our part, and can be rectified by you simply picking the baby you want from the pair if you feel you can only raise one. That solves the problem."

Caitlin's eyes widened in horror, and a flush stained her cheeks. She opened her mouth to speak, but Elizabeth spoke first. "Caitlin, take a deep breath, count to ten, think before you say anything. We're guests in this country, dear, who are being allowed to adopt these wonderful children. We don't want to do anything to jeopardize the program in place. Dear.''

"Yes, I understand. Well, Dr. Yang, I think the officials in Beijing are being very...um...accommodating and I certainly appreciate being given the choices you've just presented to me.

"But, you see, I wouldn't dream of separating identical-twin sisters under any circumstances. It's a matter of...doing things just a teeny tiny bit differently in our country.

"So, sir, with heartfelt thanks, I accept being the mother of both of these girls and I'll love them to pieces and do the very best I can raising them.''

"Very good. I'll call Beijing right back and inform them of your decision.'' He turned and hurried from the room.

"Nicely done, Caitlin,'' Elizabeth said, letting out a pent-up breath. "The Chinese people place little importance on twin girls staying together in these situations. Our emphasis that they not be separated baffles them. But you did very well. Are you certain you want to do this, though?''

"Yes,'' Caitlin said, raising her chin. "I don't have a clue as to how I'll manage, but these are my daughters.''

"Okay, but we're not out of the woods yet," Elizabeth said. "We're going to run into problems at our own consulate in Guangzhou."

"Why?" Caitlin said.

"Let's not get into it now." Elizabeth smiled. "The clock is ticking away and this visit is so short. Enjoy your girls while you can today. We'll worry about the details later. I'm going to tour this room and tickle some tummies. Hello, Grace, aren't you a smiling little thing? Oh, and let me go see Emma Lin."

Elizabeth bustled off. Marsha and Bud got up to go greet the other babies, Grace waving merrily at nothing in particular as Bud carried her.

Caitlin drew a deep, steadying breath, then smiled at Matt. "Well," she said, "this is... interesting."

Matt laughed in delight. "That's a good word for it. Whew. What a shocker, huh? Hey, let's switch babies. As the official mother of twins, you've got to learn how to divide up your time and attention between them."

In a rather clumsy shuffle of blanket-sleeper-clad bundles, the switch was made.

"Hi, sweetheart," Caitlin said, smiling at the baby now on her lap. "My gosh, Matt, if it wasn't for the fact that this baby is wearing yellow and that baby has on green, I'd never know I was holding a different one from a moment ago."

"Yep," he said, narrowing his eyes as he peered at the infant on his lap. "They're identical, all right. And cute? I'm telling you, Caitlin, I thought the pictures of Miss M. were enough to steal a heart forever, but in person? Look at these munchkins. They are really something."

"I know." Caitlin blinked back fresh tears. "I'm thrilled. No, I'm terrified. No, I'm so happy I'm... No, I'm out of my mind. Oh, dear, I'm losing it. Matt, what do you think Elizabeth meant about there being problems at our own consulate?"

"I don't have a clue, but put it out of your mind for now. Elizabeth Kane obviously knows all the ins and outs of this stuff. She'll take care of whatever obstacle there might be in Guangzhou. I'm sure she will. Just enjoy seeing and holding your daughters in the time we have left. I will never forget this day, that's for certain."

Caitlin laughed. "Oh, it's etched indelibly in my mind, too." She smiled at the baby on her lap. "And my heart. Somehow, this is all going to work out just fine. I don't know how, but it will. I'm the mother of six-month-old twin girls." Her hold on the baby tightened. "Oh, dear heaven, I'm the mother of six-month-old twin girls. The *single* mother of said twins."

Matt laughed. "Yep, you are. Keep saying it until it really sinks in. No, maybe you'd better not right now, or you might get hysterical. Hey, look at the bright side, Caitlin. You don't have to pick between the names Mackenzie and Madison. You need both of those names and it's just a matter of deciding who is who.''

"Well, that's true, isn't it?'' she said, smiling. "They're Madison Olivia and Mackenzie Olivia Cunningham. Perfect.'' She sighed. "The only problem is how do I tell them apart?''

Chapter Seven

By the time the group gathered to have dinner in the restaurant in the hotel that evening, word had spread about Caitlin's twins. Some of the parents had been so engrossed in their own new daughter, besides dealing with raging emotions, that they had been oblivious. Everyone who had brought diapers that would fit the twins offered to give Caitlin as many as they thought they could possibly spare.

Elizabeth, who was starting to appear weary, spoke quietly to each couple and Caitlin, moving around the crowded table after saying she didn't have time to eat dinner. She asked them all individually if they were comfortable with the match, with their new daughter.

"Daughters, in your case, Caitlin," Elizabeth said, smiling. "I have to ask this question officially before you sign the adoption papers this evening. Do you wish to adopt the twin girls you were matched with?"

"Yes," Caitlin said, not hesitating for one second. "Oh, yes, Elizabeth, I do."

"Fine. I've been giving this some thought. My first reaction was to say that we would switch rooms around so I was next to yours and be available to help you…because you *are* going to need assistance during the next days and nights. However, that's not a viable idea because I have tons of paperwork to take care of each evening after we have taken one step, then the next, in the process we must follow here."

"I understand," Caitlin said, nodding.

"So, how's this?" Elizabeth went on. "Matt, I realize you were recruited to help Caitlin with her luggage and what have you, but it's apparent that you have experience with babies. I know you and Caitlin just met, but you do seem to be getting along just fine and…well, I spoke to the manager of the hotel and we can move the two of you to a suite with a living room and two separate bedrooms.

"If you're willing, Matt, you would be right there when Caitlin needs help. Plus, if you could put distance between the cribs, you'd have a fighting chance that the crying of one wouldn't wake the other. What do you think?''

''Fine with me,'' Matt said.

''Caitlin?'' Elizabeth said.

Share a hotel suite with Matt? Caitlin thought, her mind racing. Yes, it was a great idea that would enable her to have an extra pair of hands when she had on her mommy hat.

But what about when she was wearing her woman hat?

Matt MacAllister sleeping on the other side of a wall? Matt sitting close by as she fed one baby and he the other? Matt functioning in the role of father as she was performing as a mother, giving the appearance that they were a true-blue family?

No.

No, this wasn't going to work, not at all.

She'd already shared kisses with Matt that had caused her to desire him, want to make love with him, with an intensity like none she'd ever known before.

She'd already daydreamed far too often about what it might be like to be the wife of a man like Matt, see him daily in his role of husband, and as the father to Mackenzie or…no, *and*…Madison.

She was already struggling to keep her confused emotions, her unsettled feelings about Matt at bay. She couldn't share a hotel suite with him. No.

''Excuse me,'' Bud said, bringing Caitlin from

her near-frantic thoughts. "I couldn't help but overhear what you said, Elizabeth, and I'm afraid I have to get into my doctor mode and object to that plan. Matt, you're on a medical leave of absence from your job. As your physician I have to voice my concerns about you being in a continual high-stress situation that twins produce by the simple fact that there are two of them."

"Now, wait a minute, Bud," Matt said.

"No, no, he's right," Elizabeth agreed. "I didn't know about your personal circumstances, Matt, and you must listen to your doctor." She shook her head. "Not only that, but now that I force my exhausted brain to work, I realize I'm running right over the top of you and Caitlin without thinking the situation through.

"There's a big jump from two people getting along together since the moment they met and that pair sharing a hotel suite, for heaven's sake. I apologize to you both. I'll figure out a better solution to this problem."

"May I have the floor?" Matt asked. "First of all, Bud, taking care of babies is not stressful to me. I'm a MacAllister, remember? I've been toting little ones around since I was a kid.

"I'm not saying that I'm eligible for the Father of the Year Award, because the needs of six-month-old infants are creature comforts, don't require the know-how of what to say to a child who, for example, got slugged by the bully at school. That part is out of my league.

"But help tend to Madison and Mackenzie? I can handle that without getting my blood pressure or ulcer in an uproar." Matt paused. "As far as sharing a suite with Caitlin? It makes more sense than being in rooms with a connecting door because it offers more space with the living room. I say we should go with the plan."

"You've convinced me," Bud said, then shifted his attention to Marsha, who was asking him a question.

"Caitlin?" Elizabeth said. "What do you think about this?"

"What? Oh, I was just mulling over what all of you said, Elizabeth. Matt's already on the other side of a wall, isn't he?"

"Pardon me?" Elizabeth said.

"Never mind. I agree to your plan, Elizabeth. Thank you for your willingness to help, Matt."

"No problem," he said, smiling.

Caitlin switched her attention back to Elizabeth.

"What did you mean, Elizabeth, when you said there was an obstacle at our embassy about the twins?"

"I'm the one who informs the embassy about how many visas we need for the babies to leave China. Since I didn't know about the twins, either, they're only prepared to issue you, a single mother, one entry visa. They will have gotten approval from our INS to do that and they have no authority to issue another visa because of the twins.''

''Oh, my gosh, what are we going to do?'' Caitlin asked.

''Not panic. I don't want to discuss the situation over the telephone with the man in charge, my longtime friend, Brian Hudson. I'd rather wait until I can plead our case in person when we arrive in Guangzhou in a few days. *Don't worry.* We'll find a loophole we can wiggle through somewhere.

''An emergency-need visa could be issued by Brian, but the stickler might be that you're a single woman requesting the INS to allow you to raise two babies at once. No one who is involved in international adoptions is allowed, as you've been told, to use any government-funded programs in the United States such as reduced-rate day care, free medical clinics, food-supplement distribution facilities and so on.''

''I see,'' Caitlin said slowly. ''So, our INS might view me as financially, or physically, unable to tend to the girls alone.''

Elizabeth nodded. ''That's the hurdle we have to get over. But my mighty brain is working on it. Let me do the stewing. You and Matt get ready to pamper and please Mackenzie and Madison.''

Elizabeth paused and reached into her purse. ''Oh, I almost forgot. I packed a bottle of nail polish to match my red dress for the big shebang we have the last night in China.'' She handed the bottle to Caitlin. ''This will save at least part of your sanity. Paint one of the babies' toenails or finger-nails red so you can tell them apart.''

''Thank you. What a fantastic idea.''

''Like I said,'' Elizabeth said, tapping one tem-ple with a fingertip. ''Mighty mind. I've got to dash. Dr. Yang is waiting for me to tell him every-one is happy with their match and he can bring the notary over tonight to take care of the next step in the paperwork. Bye for now.''

''Bye,'' Caitlin said absently. She sighed as she stared at the bright bottle of nail polish she was holding. ''Red. I only have one little red dress for the celebration dinner. How can I possibly pick one of the babies over the other to wear it?

''Oh, never mind. What a ridiculous thing to be stewing about when you consider everything I have to be concerned with regarding my daughters. For example, the matter of being one visa short.''

''Elizabeth will tend to that,'' Matt said. ''You go ahead and worry about little red dresses like a dedicated mommy should.''

A flash of anger consumed Caitlin and she glanced quickly around the table, seeing that no one was paying the least bit of attention to her and Matt before she spoke to him again.

''You know, Mr. Sunshine, your laid-back, look-at-the-bright-side, the-glass-is-half-full malarkey is starting to come across as very condescending, especially since I know that your life-is-just-a-bowl-of-cherries spiel is as phony as a three-dollar bill.''

Matt's eyes widened. "What?"

"You heard me," Caitlin said, lifting her chin.

"I'm condescending, and phony as a three-dollar bill?"

"At times." She nodded. "Well, ha to your nothing-bothers-me-so-quit-being-so-neurotic-Caitlin bit, because it is wearing thin.

"You seem to be forgetting that I know you are under Bud's care for stress and the symptoms thereof. You may put on a good front, but you obviously internalize what is bothering you. I may end up with more worry-wrinkle lines than you, but at least I'm healthy because I express my concerns."

"Well, I'm just sorry to hell and back for attempting to relieve some of your anxieties, Ms. Cunningham," Matt said, his jaw tightening. "Okay, try this on for size and see if you like it better. I have a knot of fear in my gut the size of Toledo that Elizabeth won't be able to pull enough strings to get another entry visa, and you'll be forced to leave one those babies behind.

"And, Caitlin? If that happens, a part of my heart will be left here, too, because both of those sweethearts grabbed hold of it and won't let go. I can't even imagine how you, their mother, will feel if it actually happens that way. How's that for gloom and doom? Am I getting it? Do I pass the think-the-worst test?''

Matt shook his head. ''Man, if I ever have a son I'm going to tell him early on that he'll never understand women no matter how hard he tries.''

''Hey, Caitlin and Matt,'' Marsha said from across the table, ''what am I missing over there? You both look angry enough to chew nails. Care to share?''

''No,'' Caitlin and Matt said in unison.

''Marsha,'' Bud said, ''that's your cue to mind your own business.''

''It's perfectly understandable,'' one of the women said, ''that Caitlin and Matt, that any of us, for that matter, might be a bit touchy, edgy, at the moment.

''Between still having some jet lag and being on emotional overload about the babies, our nerves are just shot to blue blazes. Before we came down for dinner I snapped at Sam because he was channel surfing on the television and wasn't in the bathroom taking his shower so he could dress for dinner.''

''The clincher being,'' Sam said, laughing, ''I'd taken my shower and dressed before Mary Ellen did and she'd completely spaced out, didn't register it at all.''

"Right," Mary Ellen said. "I was sitting there going over every second of our time spent with our Holly at the orphanage and was totally unaware of what Sam was doing. So whatever you're fussing about, Caitlin and Matt, try to put it aside, because none of us are operating on all cylinders at the moment."

A flush of embarrassment stained Caitlin's cheeks and she dipped her head to smooth the napkin she'd placed across her lap.

Marsha laughed merrily. "I barked at Bud for putting the diapers in the drawer wrong side up, so they'd have to be flipped over when we use them. I mean, the man should go to jail for such a transgression, people. That was a major crime."

Laughter erupted around the table, with everyone joining in except Caitlin, who was staring off to the left, and Matt, who directed his attention in the opposite direction.

"Well, this was fun," Marsha said, pushing back her chair, "but I'm exhausted. After we're called to gather, and have signed whatever those papers are that Elizabeth was talking about, I'm going to go crawl in bed and finish the novel I packed and read most of on the plane. Good night, all."

The others nodded in agreement to being tired and got to their feet just as a man hurried to the table.

"Caitlin and Matt, please?" he said.

"Yes?" Caitlin said.

"Here are the key packets to the suite," the man said. "Your belongings have been moved for you already and another crib brought in to accommodate your twins."

"Thank you so much," Caitlin said, taking the packets and extending one to Matt without looking at him. "You're most kind."

"We are happy to please. The little girls you fine people are taking to America are lucky babies. Yes, lucky babies. Oh, and Ms. Elizabeth Kane asks that you all come to her room, which is number 419, at seven o'clock to sign documents. Thank you." He turned and bustled away.

"That gives us a half hour," Marsha said. "Bud, let's go into that little store off the lobby and buy some postcards."

"I thought you were exhausted," Bud said, following Marsha as she started away.

"Never too tired to shop, my sweet."

As the group started toward the door, Caitlin got quickly to her feet. "I'm going to the room and make certain that the diapers aren't upside down in the drawer," she said, then hurried after the others.

Matt sat alone at the table, absently drawing lines on the tablecloth with the end of a spoon, a deep frown on his face.

Well, he thought with a sigh, Caitlin could certainly be brutally frank when she got on a rip about something. He was condescending? Phony as a three-dollar bill with his cheerful-to-the-max persona? Talk about a pop in the chops.

But the thing was…she was right.

He had worked very hard over the years to master the technique of staying up, being the MacAllister cheerleader through the various crises the family faced. He'd fine-tuned that ability until it came naturally, just slid into place when he needed it.

And he did it better than any other MacAllister.

Exiting the restaurant, Matt wandered down the block, finally coming to a small park where he slouched onto a bench, crossing his feet at the ankles. He blanked his mind and watched the never-ending maze of bicycles versus automobiles in the street within his view.

Time lost meaning as he sat there aware only of the fact that he had never before felt so alone…and lonely.

After signing the papers as instructed, Caitlin went back to the suite that she and Matt would now be sharing with Mackenzie and Madison, fully expecting him to have returned by then. She intended to apologize to him for her rude and completely unreasonable remarks about him being so damnably cheerful about everything.

When she realized that Matt still hadn't come

upstairs, she sank onto the sofa in the living room and stared at the door, willing him to appear.

Dear heaven, she thought miserably, she hated, just hated, the fact that she and Matt were at odds, had had an honest-to-goodness argument...which was all her fault. She'd been so witchy. What kind of woman hollered at a man because he had a positive outlook toward life? A cuckoo woman, that's what kind.

She didn't blame Matt for not wanting to come to the suite in fear that she'd find some fault with him for...for what? Being willing to lose sleep and put out energy to help her with the babies?

Matt hadn't hesitated for even a heartbeat when he'd agreed to move into this suite and change his share of diapers. Oh, that was so sweet, so dear, so wonderful.

Caitlin's eyes filled with tears and she sniffled.

Matt was as worried as she was about the visa for the second baby, her mind rushed on. He'd said, in so many words, that Mackenzie and Madison had stolen his heart and he would be devastated if one of them had to be left behind. And he'd said that if *he* felt that way, he could only imagine how *she* must feel and...

He was so sensitive. So caring. So assured of his own masculinity that he had no qualms about expressing the fact that tiny babies had turned him into a puddle of putty. Not every man on this earth would be willing to do that. But Matt had.

And she'd told him he was as phony as a three-dollar bill.

"Oh-h-h," Caitlin said, "I can't stand myself. I'm an awful person, just awful. Matt, please come back so I can tell you how sorry I am. Please."

Caitlin sniffled again, stared at the door...and waited.

Just after midnight, Caitlin jerked awake, wondering where on earth she was. In the next three seconds she registered three facts—she had fallen asleep on the sofa in the living room of the suite, she'd been wakened by the sound of Matt opening the door and he was now walking slowly toward her.

Caitlin jumped to her feet, ran across the room, grabbed handfuls of Matt's shirt and looked into his wide-with-shock eyes.

"Oh, Matt," she said, "I'm so sorry for being so nasty. I apologize and I'm begging you to forgive me. To think I was criticizing you for having a bright outlook toward life and... There's no excuse for the terrible things I said to you. None.

"Your willingness to move into this suite and help me with the babies is so giving, so caring, and I should be thanking you a thousand times instead of...

"I don't care if the others were laughing about how crabby everyone is because we're all on emotional overload, that doesn't erase my need to tell you how wrong I was and how very, very sorry I am. Forgive me? Please?"

"I'll forgive you, Caitlin," Matt said, sliding his arms around her back, "on one condition."

"Just name it."

"That you forgive me."

"Forgive you? But you didn't do anything wrong."

"Yes, I did," he said with a sigh. "I've thought about this for hours as I sat in a little park near here. I tried to figure out a way to apologize to you without baring my soul, explain that I... But I finally came to the conclusion that there's no way to make it sensible without doing just that...bare my soul. Let's sit down."

They sat on the sofa, Matt shifting so he could take both of Caitlin's hands in his as he looked directly into her eyes. "Okay, here I go. The tale of woe of Matt MacAllister." He paused. "Caitlin, the MacAllisters are a fantastic family of overachievers who do things to the max and do them with excellence. While I was growing up I continually fell short. I wasn't as smart, wasn't as athletic, wasn't receiving awards for this and that. In my eyes, I didn't measure up."

"Oh, Matt, no, you're—"

"Let me finish, because this isn't easy for me to do."

Caitlin nodded.

"I'm not certain when I started doing it…maybe as far back as high school even, but I adopted a facade of go with the flow, give the appearance of always knowing that everything would be fine no matter what was going on, did my glass-is-half-full routine ad nauseam until I had it perfected. And it worked. I became known in the family as the one to go to with problems because good ole Matt just always seemed to make things better, sent you on your way with a pocketful of sunshine and a belief that all would be well.

"I was better at it than any other MacAllister, finally had something that set me apart, made me top-notch in an arena no one else could come close to matching."

"I understand," Caitlin said softly.

"The thing is," he went on, "I don't know how to turn it off when I should. Every woman I've ever been involved with has eventually complained that I don't really listen to what she is saying, I just wait for her to shut up so I can whip out one of my cheerful clichés and end the discussion.

"I dismissed those criticisms as being female logic I couldn't comprehend, the relationship would end, and I'd go merrily on my way. I finally got tired of arguments on the subject and haven't dated much in the past few years.

"I realized I was in another position to be the best, to measure up to MacAllister standards. My job at the hospital. So I dived into it, buried myself in that place, lived it, breathed it, until I wrecked my health. But what the hell, I was the best at what I did."

"Oh, Matt," Caitlin said, shaking her head.

"But tonight?" he went on. "When you, too, accused me of just glossing over problems, dismissing them with a breezy, corny platitude, I couldn't handle your being angry, disgusted with me, because you mean too much to me, Caitlin. I've never told anyone, not anyone, what I just revealed to you, but I hope that by your knowing you'll find it in your heart to forgive me."

Caitlin searched her mind frantically for the words that would express how deeply touched she was that Matt had shared what he had with her, how very special she felt, how consumed she was with a foreign warmth like nothing she'd ever experienced before. But those words stayed just beyond her reach.

She pulled her hands from beneath his, framed his face, then leaned forward and kissed him, hoping that somehow that kiss would convey her heartfelt emotions.

A groan rumbled in Matt's chest and heat rocketed throughout his body. Without breaking the kiss, he scooped Caitlin onto his lap, wrapped his arms around her and deepened the kiss, his tongue delving into the sweet darkness of her mouth.

Caitlin shifted her hands to the back of Matt's neck, inching her fingers into the depths of his thick, dark auburn hair.

Matt cared for her, she thought hazily, just as she cared for him. He'd cared and he'd shared his innermost secrets with her. It didn't mean, oh no, that he could, or would, change how he conducted his life, but the fact that he wanted her to understand him, know who he was and why, was so important, so wondrous.

This night, her mind hummed in a misty place of passion, was separate and apart from reality or reason. She didn't want to think, to dwell, about the right or wrong of her desire for Matt, nor give one second of thought to the consequences she would have to face at dawn's light.

All she wanted was Matt MacAllister.

Caitlin broke the kiss and spoke close to Matt's lips, her voice trembling with need.

"I want you, Matt," she said. "I want to make love with you. I've never done anything so brazen, so… What you shared with me means so much and it belongs to this night, this stolen night out of time. Tomorrow doesn't exist, not now. There is only this night.''

"Ah, Caitlin," Matt said, his voice raspy. "Are you sure? I couldn't deal with your anger and I sure as hell couldn't handle your having regrets if we—"

"Shh. I promise. No regrets. It's one night. *Our* night."

But what about the nights yet to come? Matt's mind hammered. What about the strange yet awesome…whatever-it-was that was happening between them? Just this night, one night, was theirs? But…

"Do you want me, Matt?" Caitlin whispered. "Do you want this to be *our* night? Together?"

Matt captured Caitlin's lips in a scaring kiss, pushing aside the raging questions in his mind, refusing to address them, to give them the power to diminish what he wanted, needed, was going to share, with Caitlin.

He lifted his head, got to his feet with Caitlin held tightly in his arms and crossed the room to one of the bedrooms where a soft light glowed from the lamp on the nightstand.

He registered absently that this was Caitlin's room as he saw her belongings. He set her on her feet next to the bed, swept back the blankets to reveal crisp white sheets, then looked directly into the depths of her fathomless dark eyes, drowning in them, savoring the sensation of somehow flowing into the very essence of who she was, holding nothing of himself back.

"I cherish you," he said, hardly recognizing the gritty sound of his own voice. "I respect and admire you. And, oh, Caitlin, how I want you."

As though standing outside of herself in a dreamy mist, Caitlin watched as her clothes and Matt's seem to float from their bodies, removed by a gentle, invisible hand. She saw herself smile, oh, what a womanly smile, as she drank in the sight of the magnificent man standing before her, and gloried in the heat of his gaze and the approval radiating from his dark brown eyes.

Matt reached up and drew one thumb over her lips, and Caitlin shivered from the sensuous foray, coming back into herself so as not to miss one exquisite moment of this night. Their night. Hers and Matt's.

He lifted her into his arms again, laid her in the center of the bed, then followed her down, catching his weight on one forearm.

They touched with caresses that were as soft as feathers, exploring, discovering, marveling in all that they found, all that would be theirs, given to them in total abandon and received with reverence. Where hands had trailed a heated path, lips followed, igniting flames of passion burning.

When Caitlin could bear no more, when a sob of need caught in her throat and Matt's name whimpered from her lips, he left her only long enough to take steps to protect her, then returned to her, having been gone far, far too long.

Matt moved over her. Into her. Filling her. Then began the rocking rhythm that built in intensity to a pounding force that caused them to cling tightly to each other as they were carried up and away, searching for the summit of their glorious climb, arriving there a heartbeat apart, shattering into a million brightly colored pieces of ecstasy.

"Matt!"

"Caitlin. *Caitlin.*"

They hovered, swaying, memorizing, drifting slowly back, so slowly, gathering the shards of the very essences of their being to become themselves again, whole yet changed, never to be quite the same again.

Matt shifted to Caitlin's side, then nestled her to him, sifting his fingers through her silky hair. She splayed one hand on the moist hair on his muscled chest, feeling his heart regain a normal rhythm beneath her palm.

Then their hands stilled as sleep crept over them like a soft, comforting blanket...and they slept.

Chapter Eight

Caitlin woke the next morning to the sound of water running in the shower in the connecting bathroom between her bedroom and Matt's. She turned her head to look at the pillow next to her that still held a slight indentation of his head.

Memories of the exquisite lovemaking shared with Matt the night before tumbled through her mind, and a soft smile formed on her lips.

She had no regrets about making love with Matt, she mused dreamily. None. It had been a stolen night, a gift to herself that she would always cherish. Granted, her actions had been very out of character, far from her normal behavior, but she didn't care.

Today, on this incredibly unbelievable day, she would officially become a mother of twin baby girls when she and Matt walked out of that orphanage carrying Mackenzie and Madison. Her life would be changed forever, and she could hardly wait to learn what time they were all going to pick up their daughters. Today she put on her mother hat, firmly anchoring it in place.

But last night? She had been wearing her woman hat and…how deliciously naughty…nothing else. She had experienced the most beautiful, awesome lovemaking of her limited experience and she intended to keep the memories of what she'd shared with Matt tucked safely away in a special chamber of her heart.

Her heart, Caitlin thought, frowning. She must remember, must not forget, that her heart belonged to her daughters. She cared for Matt MacAllister, she truly did, but she mustn't allow him to stake a claim on her heart, cause her to lose a part of it to him. No.

Matt had told her his most innermost secrets last night and she was deeply touched that he had.

But knowing what motivated Matt didn't mean that he intended to change his ways.

The water in the shower stopped, then Caitlin could hear Matt moving around the bedroom on the other side of the bathroom. A few minutes later he appeared in the doorway of her bedroom.

"Good morning," he said quietly.

Caitlin smiled. "Hello. Oh, Matt, this is it. The day I become a mother. I still have flashes of not really believing that my dream has come true. Well, I guess I'll believe it when both babies are here in the suite crying at the same time, or whatever. I wonder when we're going to go to the orphanage and—"

"Caitlin," Matt interrupted, no hint of a smile on his face.

"Yes?"

"You promised me that you'd have no regrets about last night," he said, shoving his hands into the pockets of his slacks. "I need...I need to know that you're really all right about what...about...you know."

Caitlin sat up, clutching the sheet to cover her bare breasts.

"I'm fine. I'm keeping my promise. I have no regrets about making love with you, Matt. None. It was beautiful, very special, and I intend to keep the memories of it in a...treasure chest, as corny as that may sound. So, please, don't give another thought to the possibility that I'm sorry about the step we took, because I'm not."

Caitlin flopped back onto the pillow and laughed.

"And today I become a mother of twins. Maybe you should take a peek at the door and see if Elizabeth taped a note to it about what time we're going to the orphanage. No, I suppose she'll call all of us when she knows. But, oh goodness, I hope we don't have to wait all day. You know, not go until this evening. I'll be a basket case if that's how it's scheduled.''

Matt raised one hand in a halting gesture. "Wait a minute, Caitlin. Could we back up here a tad? I realize you're excited about getting the babies today, but I want to be certain that I'm understanding you correctly.''

"About what?"

"Last night." Matt stepped closer and sat down on the bed near the foot. "What we shared is a distant memory already that you've put in some imaginary treasure chest? In this, the light of the morning after, it's old news and you're thinking only about the babies? Am I getting this right?''

"What you seem to be getting," Caitlin said, sitting up again, "is angry. Why? I'm totally confused by how you're acting, Matt.''

Matt dragged both hands down his face and laughed, a strange sound that held no humor. "So am I. Confused. You kept your word, you have no regrets, yet a part of me wants to say whoa, don't dust off what we shared so quickly, don't tuck it away, or whatever, because it was so sensational, so... There were emotions intertwined with the physical beauty of it, Caitlin, and I want to know what those emotions are, what they mean, and—''

"I don't. It was a stolen night, Matt. One night. Yes, it was wonderful. Yes, there were emotions involved, but there's no point in examining them closely because…well, there just isn't. This is a new day. This is the day I become a mother and I can't, won't, think about anything other than that. As centered as you are on your job when you're in Ventura, you can surely understand tunnel vision about something."

"Sure," Matt said, forcing a lightness to his voice as he got to his feet. "I'll get out of your way and let you get ready to rock and roll and become a mommy. Do you want to eat breakfast downstairs, or shall we be indulgent and order room service?"

"Oh, let's go downstairs. Maybe some of the others will be there, or even Elizabeth herself, and we'll learn when we're going to go pick up the babies."

"Right," Matt said, then turned and walked slowly from the room, pulling the door closed behind him.

Caitlin frowned as she stared at the closed door.

Matt was acting strangely, she thought. It was as though he wanted what they'd shared last night to stay front-row center in their minds.

Good grief, men were complicated creatures, she thought as she left the bed.

In the living room of the suite, Matt stared out one of the windows, not really seeing what was within his view.

What in the hell was the matter with him? he thought, frowning. Caitlin had kept her promise.

But the burning in his gut and the pounding in his head told him that he wasn't handling her behavior well at all. He was stressed to the max, wired, was being assaulted by an amalgam of emotions that were tumbling through his mind, twisting and turning, and driving him nuts.

What did he want from Caitlin? Would he have preferred that she greet him this morning with a dewy-eyed expression and the declaration that because their lovemaking had been so wonderful they must surely be falling in love with each other, had a future together, might even... Gosh, Matt, get married and raise the twins together? They could be a family, the four of them, and live happily ever after in Ventura and—

"No," Matt said, shaking his head.

No, that was *not* what he wanted to hear Caitlin say, because he wasn't ready for that lifestyle, that kind of commitment to hearth, home, babies and forever. Granted, he was going to have to ease up on his hours at the hospital, but his job there was still where he was centered, with room for little else in his existence.

Was this a disgusting male thing? he wondered. An issue of control? Did he want Caitlin to fall at his feet so he could go into testosterone overload and lecture her on how she had to keep her promise, that what they'd shared was over, done, finished, by golly, and no womanly fantasies of a wedding and instant fatherhood had any place in this scenario?

He'd declared the terms and she was to follow them, by damn. One night. No more. End of story. So, knock it off, Caitlin.

Oh, surely he wasn't that shallow, that caught up in flexing his male ego. No, what he was was terribly confused as to why he'd felt such a chilling emptiness, then anger, then hurt, then that hollowness again, as he heard Caitlin chatter on about today and getting the babies, while last night was already tucked away in a treasure chest or some such thing.

"You're losing it, MacAllister," he said aloud. "So find it and get it together. Right now."

By the time Caitlin emerged from the bedroom in blue slacks and a white blouse with blue flowers, Matt had managed to push aside the mangled mess in his mind and shift mental gears to match Caitlin's focus on the twins.

"I wonder," he said, "if we're supposed to take clothes to change the babies into before we leave the orphanage with them? I don't think they can afford to allow anything they have to be given away."

"That's a good thought," Caitlin said, nodding. "But I'm sure Elizabeth will tell us. She's done this so many times she probably can recite all the details without a second thought. Shall we go have some breakfast? I hope there's room in my stomach for food, because right now there are a whole bunch of butterflies fluttering around in there.''

Matt smiled. ''Let's go feed the butterflies.''

About half of the group had already eaten by the time Caitlin and Matt reached the lobby of the hotel. Others, including Marsha and Bud, were heading for the restaurant and Caitlin and Matt joined them.

The conversation at the table during the meal was about babies, rattled nerves, wondering where Elizabeth was, confessions of hardly being able to sleep the night before because of what would transpire on this day, and on and on.

''Have you figured out how you'll decide which of your girls is Madison and which is Mackenzie, Caitlin?'' Marsha said as they all lingered over one more cup of coffee.

Caitlin nodded.

''The caregivers will hand one baby to me, and one to Matt. The one I hold first is Madison.''

''Oh, I like that,'' Marsha said. ''It's as though you were giving birth to them. You know, the one who is born first is Madison. You're very clever, Caitlin.'' She paused and looked at the pitcher on the table. ''Do I want more coffee? No, better not. My nerves are edgy enough.''

It was as though Caitlin was giving birth to the twins, Matt mentally repeated. She wasn't, of course. But Marsha's statement had brought him full circle back to the night he'd met Caitlin and how he had wondered why she was taking the momentous step of adopting a baby from China and becoming a single mother.

It still didn't make much sense. Caitlin was an attractive, intelligent, fun to be with, and...yes, passionate woman that any man would be fortunate to have as his life partner, his soul mate, his wife and the mother of his children. He couldn't believe that Caitlin was here in China to gain the title of mother due to lack of opportunity to marry and have children in the conventional manner.

She skittered around the answer when he'd asked her why she'd chosen this path, had obviously not wished to share it with him.

Man, things were sure lopsided at the moment, he mused. He'd bared his soul to Caitlin last night, told her things about himself that no one, *no one,* knew. Maybe now, or at the exact right moment, she'd be willing to divulge *her* secret.

It was...okay...it was important to him that she trusted him enough to do that. Why? Hell, there was another unanswered question to throw on the towering heap.

"Headache, Matt?" Bud said, bringing Matt from his tangled thoughts. "You're rubbing your forehead."

"What? Oh, no, I'm fine. I had a little headache,

but the caffeine in the coffee is taking care of it. Bring on the babies. I'm ready.''

"Aren't we all?" Marsha said. "I'll never survive if Elizabeth says we're not picking them up until tonight or something grim like that.''

"I already had that thought," Caitlin said. "What if Elizabeth is still snoozing away in her room because she knows nothing is going to happen this morning?"

"Elizabeth," Bud said, jumping to his feet and nearly knocking over his chair. "I just caught a glimpse of her in the lobby.''

"Well, my goodness," Marsha said, rising. "Don't you dare say another word about me being wound up to the point of ridiculous. You just scared the bejeebers out of all of us.''

Bud laughed. "Sorry about that. I've never been a father before, and today is the day I become one. This, people, is scary stuff.''

"You're going to be a super dad." Marsha kissed him on the cheek.

"And I'm going to be a super temporary daddy," Matt said, getting to his feet and extending one hand to Caitlin. "Feel free to call on me for advice as needed, Bud.''

Caitlin rose and smiled up at Matt, who was still holding her hand. "On behalf of Madison and Mackenzie who would otherwise be left to my inexperienced mercy," she said, "we are eternally grateful for your baby expertise, Mr. MacAllister.''

"I live to serve," Matt said, matching her smile.

They continued to look directly into each other's eyes, suddenly oblivious to those around them. Heat from their clasped hands traveled up and through them, igniting the embers of desire that still glowed from the previous night.

"Um," Marsha said, stifling a giggle, "I hate to interrupt, but are you two ready to go into the lobby and see if Elizabeth is still there and if she has any news?"

"What?" Matt said, dropping Caitlin's hand. "Oh, sure thing."

"Yes, of course," Caitlin said, spinning around. "Off we go."

In the lobby Elizabeth welcomed those emerging from the restaurant, then narrowed her eyes as she looked at the entire group. "Okay, good," she said finally. "Everyone is here. I just spoke with Dr. Yang, and the vans are on the way to pick us up to go to the orphanage. This, as they say, is it."

Excited chatter broke out, gaining volume until Elizabeth raised one hand for silence.

"You'll be bringing your daughters back here in their clothes from the orphanage, but we need to return those clothes later, as they can't be spared. Please have them laundered by the service here in the hotel, then you can bring them to my room when they're fresh and clean again.

"We have no appointments scheduled for today, so you can spend the hours getting to know the newest member of your family. By the time we get back, pitchers of hot water will have been brought to your rooms so that you can make formula.

"I urge you to talk to your daughter as much as possible so she gets used to the sound of your voice, which will have a very different pitch than what she's used to.

"If she fusses if you hold her for any length of time, don't be upset. You must remember that these babies haven't been held a great deal as there simply aren't enough caregivers to go around at the orphanage. Sometimes, though, they come to enjoy being held so much they pitch a fit when you put them down. You just never know. Any questions?"

"Only about a million," Bud said, smiling. "But I guess the bottom line is…we wing it."

Elizabeth laughed. "That's right on the money. Just do the best you can. If you feel there is a medical problem, call my room and we'll take it from there." She glanced over her shoulder. "The vans are here. Is everyone ready to go?"

Caitlin patted her cheeks. "No. Yes. No. Oh, I'm a wreck."

"Me, too," Matt said as the group started across the lobby. "I'm not going to say everything is going to be just fine, because I'm suddenly very intimidated by the image of Madison and Mackenzie in my mind. They're about to run our show, Caitlin. They are definitely going to call the shots."

"Thank you for admitting that you're as nervous

as I am. It's very honest of you, real, and…well, thank you.''

''Honest, real and overdue.'' Matt frowned. ''Wait until my family gets a load of the new me. They'll tell me something gloomy and I'll say, 'Wow, that is really lousy. If I were you I'd be totally bummed.' They'll fall over from shock.''

''At first maybe, but I think they'll come to appreciate the new you as much…well, as much as I do.''

''Time will tell,'' Matt said, then followed Caitlin into one of the vans.

As Caitlin settled in her seat with Matt next to her, she glanced up at him quickly.

Matt really was changing, she mused. He was dropping the phony everything-is-always-rosy facade and expressing his true feelings about things.

If he could make a major adjustment like that after so many years of behaving as he had been, couldn't he also adopt a better balance in his existence between work and his personal life? If he really wanted to, couldn't he own more than one hat?

Caitlin, stop it, she ordered herself and focused on the drive to the orphanage. The streets were the usual maze of bicycles and cars, and it seemed to her that the drive was taking forever. But at last the tall structure came into view and she clutched her hands tightly in her lap.

Inside the building, they once again entered the

elevator in small numbers, then were finally all gathered in the living room where they'd been the day before. Dr. Yang appeared, smiled at everyone, then disappeared again with Elizabeth. Everyone sat statue still, hardly breathing, gazes riveted on the doorway.

"Breathe," Matt whispered in Caitlin's ear. "In. Out. Inhale. Exhale."

A funny little bubble of laughter escaped from Caitlin's lips, then she drew a deep breath.

"What's taking so long?" she said, her voice hushed.

"It's been two minutes and twenty seconds," Matt said, looking at his watch.

"It's been two years and twenty hours," she said, smiling up at him.

"Close, very close. Man, this is torture."

Elizabeth and Dr. Yang suddenly reappeared with a group of caregivers visible behind them.

"Mommies and daddies," Elizabeth said, beaming, "your daughters are ready to go home with you. Bless you all."

Names were called in the same manner as the previous day and precious bundles placed in welcoming arms.

"Caitlin Cunningham," Dr. Yang said.

Caitlin and Matt got to their feet and crossed the room. A caregiver placed a baby in a faded yellow blanket sleeper in Caitlin's arms and another in a very worn pale green sleeper in Matt's. Tears filled

Caitlin's eyes as she looked at the infant who was staring up at her.

"Hello, Madison," she said. "Hello. I'm your mommy." She gazed at the baby Matt was holding. "And you are Mackenzie. I'm your mommy, Mackenzie." She sniffled. "Who is falling apart. Oh, Matt, aren't they wonderful?"

When Matt didn't answer, she looked up at him. Her breath caught and her heart seemed to skip a beat as she saw the tears glistening in Matt's eyes.

"Yeah," he said, his voice gritty. "They're really something. We're holding miracles, Caitlin. Do you realize that? There aren't words to express... Whew.

"Let's go sit down and see if we can get these little ladies to smile at us again. What do you say, Madison and Mackenzie? Do you have smiles to share with your mommy and your...well, I qualify for now. How about a smile for your daddy, too?"

Chapter Nine

At midnight that night *no one* in the Cunningham-MacAllister suite in the hotel was smiling.

The day had flown by and Caitlin couldn't remember when she'd been so consumed with pure joy as she and Matt worked side by side tending to the babies.

She painted Madison's toenails with the bright red polish, then she and Matt bathed the girls, supporting their backs so they could sit up in the tub and splash to their heart's content, resulting in the adults having to change into dry tops.

After consuming bottles down to the last drop of the formula Caitlin prepared, the babies took long naps in the cribs that were standing end to end in the living room.

At dinnertime Matt ordered room service, and he and Caitlin ate while watching the twins as they lay on their tummies on a blanket on the floor. They could both hold their heads up and reach for the small toys Caitlin had tucked along the edges of her suitcase.

They played with the babies after dinner until they began to fuss, then changed them into blanket sleepers, fed each a bottle and put them in the cribs, where they fell instantly asleep.

Exhausted but happy, Caitlin bid Matt good-night, then went to her room, leaving the door open halfway so she could be certain to hear the infants if they cried. Matt watched *Casablanca* on television with the characters all speaking Chinese in voice-overs that didn't match the movement of their mouths, which he found strangely entertaining, then headed for bed about ten o'clock.

At 10:32, only seconds apart, both girls began to cry. Caitlin nearly flew into the living room, wearing a full-length white granny nightgown, and Matt came barreling out of his room after pulling on his slacks but not stopping long enough for a shirt.

Diapers were changed. Bottles were offered and firmly refused. The twins wailed on, louder and louder. Caitlin and Matt began to walk the floor, each patting an unhappy bundle on the back and

speaking in soothing tones. Madison and Mackenzie cried, and cried and cried.

At midnight, Caitlin sank onto the sofa with
Mackenzie in her arms and continued to pat her on
the back. Matt settled next to her with a weary sigh,
Madision matching her sister's volume of distress.

"Oh, my gosh," Caitlin said, loud enough to be
heard above the din. "What on earth can be the
matter with them? They were fine all day, Matt.
Are they sick? In pain? How can they cry so hard
for so long and not run out of oxygen? What's
wrong with them?"

"I don't know," he said, rubbing Madison's
back as he propped her against one shoulder.
"Don't even have a clue."

"I thought you were the expert on babies."

"That doesn't include reading their minds."

Caitlin got to her feet again and resumed her
trek, jiggling Mackenzie.

"Please, Mackenzie, don't cry," she said, then
sniffled. "Oh, I feel so helpless, so inadequate.
What if I was home right now and trying to do this
alone? Aren't I supposed to be able to figure out
what's the matter with my own daughters?" Tears
filled her eyes. "Oh, good, Caitlin, now I'll cry
right along with them, which will solve absolutely
nothing."

"I may start wailing any moment myself," Matt
said, chuckling. "This is nuts. We're two intelli-

gent adults and we're reduced to stressed-out mush by two tiny little girls.''

"It's scary, isn't it?" Caitlin laughed in spite of herself. "They are really pushing our buttons."

Matt got up, gripped Madison around the chest and held her high in the air.

"Hello up there," he said to the screaming infant. "Care to share what's wrong with you?"

Madison drew a wobbly breath, then threw up curdled formula all down the front of Matt's bare chest.

"Oh, man," Matt shouted, holding Madison straight out in front of him. "Oh, hell. Oh, yuck."

Madison kicked her feet, gurgled, then produced a big smile.

"She stopped crying," Caitlin said as Mackenzie wailed on. "She had a tummyache all this time. I bet that's what's wrong with Mackenzie, too. I diluted the formula, but it was still too rich for them. Oh, poor babies."

"Poor babies?" Matt said none too quietly as he kept Madison at arm's length. "What about me? This junk is rank, really gross."

"True. You smell rather… Never mind. Look at the bright side, which you do so well. At least you aren't wearing a shirt that has to be laundered. You have a very nice build, by the way. Very nice. I don't think I told you that when we… Changing the subject now. Would you consider holding Mackenzie up in the air like you did Madison so she might..."

"Don't even think about it," Matt said, narrowing his eyes.

"Just thought I'd ask."

Mackenzie suddenly burped. It was a loud, very unladylike belch. Then she shivered, sighed and laid her head on Caitlin's shoulder. A blessed silence fell over the room.

Matt laid Madison in her crib and she lifted her feet and grabbed her toes with her tiny hands as she made funny little noises and blew bubbles. Caitlin eased Mackenzie from her shoulder and put her in the other crib. Her lashes drifted down and she fell asleep.

"Don't make any sudden moves," Matt said, his voice hushed. "Okay, Madison, let go of the piggies and take a snooze. That's it. You can play with your toes tomorrow. Good night, good night, good night."

Madison blinked slowly several times, then drifted off in a peaceful slumber.

Caitlin and Matt peered in the cribs, hardly breathing, then looked at each other.

"What do you think?" Caitlin whispered.

"I think that if I don't go take a shower in the next three seconds I'm going to lose my dinner, too. Who invented this formula junk?"

Caitlin clamped a hand over her mouth to stifle a laugh.

"It's not funny."

"No, it isn't," Caitlin said, attempting and failing to curb a smile. "But you're the hero in this awful scenario. If you hadn't held Madison up in the air like that she probably wouldn't have... Well, you know."

"Yeah, I know." Matt chuckled. "Well, we survived our first baby crisis together. I'm off to take a shower."

"Matt," Caitlin said as he started across the room. "Thank you. I don't know what I would have done without you. You were wonderful. So patient and...well, all I can say is thank you."

"Hey," he said, turning to face her, "we're in this together. We're a team, Caitlin. There's nothing to thank me for. Okay?"

"Okay," she said, smiling at him warmly.

"By the way, do you always wear a granny gown to bed?"

"What? Oh, no. I sleep in a T-shirt at home. I bought this nightie for the trip because I didn't know how cool the nights would be, and I didn't have room in my suitcase for a robe, and I figured I'd be getting up in the night with the baby...which turned out to be two babies and..." She glanced down at her gown. "It's awful, isn't it?"

"Yes, it is. But not entirely, because I know

what's beneath that grim creation. That gown is sort of like the bulky wrapping on a hidden gift that is actually extremely exquisite. Just thought I'd mention it.''

Matt turned and strode away, disappearing into his bedroom.

''Oh. Well,'' Caitlin said, looking down at her nightie again. ''Fancy that.''

She shook her head slightly to dispel the sudden, sensuous pictures in her mind of when both she and Matt had stood naked before the other, then reached out and...

Don't go there, Caitlin.

She went to the cribs where Mackenzie and Madison were sleeping peacefully, covered each with a soft blanket, then went back to the sofa and slouched onto it, staring at the ceiling.

She was exhausted, Caitlin thought. The time spent trying to soothe the crying babies had seemed like an eternity. She'd felt so helpless, so inadequate, so useless.

Caitlin raised her head and wrapped her hands around her elbows.

If it hadn't been for Matt, she thought miserably, her daughters would probably still be crying, suffering from tummyaches caused by the formula she'd prepared.

Two tears slid down Caitlin's cheeks.

What was she going to do without Matt? She

would miss him. He'd become very important to her, very quickly. She cared for him deeply, she was willing to admit that. No, no, she wasn't in love with him, wouldn't be so foolish as to lose her heart to a man who was centered so completely on his career. She'd had enough pain in her life due to a man like that. But she *did* care for him very, very much.

When she and the babies were back in Ventura, they'd get into a workable routine, she mentally rambled on. She'd learn how to take care of them to the best of her ability and hope and pray that would be good enough. If they both cried at the same time like tonight she'd just…she'd just weep right along with them and wait for a fairy godmother to show up, wave her wand and fix whatever was wrong with Madison and Mackenzie.

Two more tears slid down Caitlin's face, but she ignored them.

Go to bed, she ordered herself. Get some sleep, much-needed sleep, while the babies were doing the same. But she didn't seem to have the energy to move, to get to her feet, shuffle into the bedroom and crawl into bed. All she was capable of doing at the moment was just sit and cry.

"Hey," Matt said.

Caitlin jerked at the sudden sound of Matt's voice, then dashed the tears from her cheeks as he sat down next to her and encircled her shoulders with one arm.

"Tears?" he said gently.

"I...I'm just tired, and I guess I'm frightened, too, Matt, because I'm so overwhelmed right now with the realization of what a momentous task I've taken on. I failed miserably tonight. I couldn't soothe or comfort them, couldn't figure out what was wrong with them or... They'd still be crying if I'd been taking care of them alone, I just know they would be."

"And you're projecting that into when you'll be home with them in Ventura."

Caitlin nodded.

"Your fears are understandable, but what I can't get a handle on is why you were determined to become a single mother in the first place."

"You're a perfect example of why I made the decision I did."

"What do you mean?"

"Suppose, just pretend for a moment that you and I fell in love and got married. This is hypothetical, of course, but you're a classic case, so I'm using you to explain my position."

"Mmm," Matt said, frowning.

"The truth of the matter would be," Caitlin went on, "that you really wouldn't be married to me but to your job, your chosen career. I lived that nightmare, Matt, and I won't do it again, nor will I allow Mackenzie and Madison to be subjected to it.''

"But…"

Caitlin got to her feet, then turned to look at Matt, wrapping her hands around her elbows.

"I won't drag the pain of my past into my present and future, relive that agony, that chilling loneliness, helplessness." Tears filled Caitlin's eyes and threatened to spill onto her pale cheeks. "I won't."

"What are you talking about?" Matt said, staring at her intently.

"My father was a doctor, a highly respected heart surgeon. People came from across the country, the world, to be his patient, to receive his expertise.

"Oh, God, I remember staring out the window waiting, waiting for him to come home to celebrate my birthday, or to go to the school play I was in, or to take me to the zoo like he promised…but he didn't come. Time after time he didn't come because one of his patients needed him and they were always more important than me, than my mother.

"And my mother? I can still see her, Matt, in her pretty, new dress, standing by the door waiting for my father to arrive so they could go out to celebrate their anniversary, or *her* birthday, or because he'd promised her that this time nothing would keep him from being there for her. But he didn't come.

"I'd hear her, Matt," Caitlin said, weeping openly, "crying behind her closed bedroom door, her heart broken yet again, just as mine was so many, many times. We never came first with him. His patients were more important. His almighty career, reputation, the power and prestige, came before his wife and child.

"He died of a heart attack when I was sixteen and I didn't even cry. Why would I? He was a stranger I hardly knew. A man who was gone before I got up in the morning and didn't return home until I was sound asleep at night. He was a shadowy figure who broke promises, made me cry, made my mother weep as he chipped away at her heart and her love for him until there was nothing left.

"Oh, I knew that all men aren't like my father, but every man I've dated put his career at the top of the list of importance."

"Ah, Caitlin."

"That's why I decided to become a single mother and adopt my child from China. Oh, sure, I daydreamed about finding a man who would put me, his children, first, have the proper balance in his existence between work and family, but I never found him. I still haven't. But I vowed I wouldn't be cheated out of my dream of being a mother, too.''

''I...I don't know what to say to you.''

''There's nothing to say, nothing,'' she said, shaking her head. ''I've got to get some sleep. I'm tired, so very tired. Good night, Matt. Thank... thank you again for your help with the babies.''

Caitlin hurried to her bedroom.

Matt drew a deep breath, let it out slowly, then rose and went to the cribs. He smoothed the blankets on the sleeping babies, then dragged both hands down his face.

Well, he thought, as they said in courtrooms, the question was asked and answered. He now knew Caitlin's secret, the reason she had been determined to become a single mother. She'd even used him as the perfect example of the type of career-oriented man she would never marry, nor allow to be a father to her daughters.

Caitlin had looked so...so sad as she'd poured out her heart to him. He'd wanted to take her into his arms, comfort her, tell her that not all men were like her father, that he, Matt MacAllister wasn't. But he'd been frozen in place, words of assurance beyond his reach.

Visions of arriving late time after time at family functions had flashed before his mind's eye, as well as when he hadn't gotten there at all because he was still tied up at the hospital. He'd seen himself finally showing up, then being so exhausted he'd added nothing to the conversations taking place.

But how did a man become the very best in his chosen career without that kind of devotion to duty? How did he continue to meet the high MacAllister standards?

Matt sighed and a few minutes later was in bed, hoping sleep would claim him quickly and give him a reprieve from the cacophony of voices in his beleaguered mind.

His thoughts floated back to the screaming crisis of earlier with Mackenzie and Madison. He'd been focused totally on Caitlin and the unhappy babies, had given the situation his complete concentration just as he did when he was working at Mercy Hospital. But how did a man give one hundred percent of himself to two completely different parts of his life?

That was the question asked and not yet answered.

But tonight? he thought, smiling into the darkness. Tonight he'd been right in there pitching with those little munchkins. Had stood by Caitlin's side as an equal partner.

His contribution to the crisis had been important, it mattered, and he'd even solved the dilemma by accident. Granted, having a six-month-old baby throw up all over him wasn't a thrill a minute, but it had done the trick and he'd felt about ten feet tall. Smelly but victorious.

He'd given Caitlin a hard time about her granny gown, he mentally rambled on, but the truth of the matter was she looked adorable, made him want to just scoop her into his arms and kiss her until they both couldn't breathe. Plus, there was the fact, as he'd told her, that he knew how exquisitely feminine she was beneath those endless folds of material.

Ah, yes, this had been a night to remember. A night that made him realize what it would be like when he got married, became a husband and father. But when would that be? When would he figure out how to balance two worlds so that no one got shortchanged? Other MacAllisters seemed to be able to do it, so what was the secret formula? What if he was never able to get a handle on it? God, what a bleak picture of his future that thought painted.

Well, forget it for now. He was in China with Caitlin and those precious babies and they had his full attention. He'd zero in on the big picture of his life when he got home.

But, damn it, he had a big enough challenge facing him when he returned to Ventura. He had to continue to excel at his job, be the best, without further damaging his health. That was going to take his full concentration as he learned to delegate, cut back on his hours a little…okay, more than a little…while still maintaining his reputation as being top-notch, one of the leaders in his field.

"Enough of this," Matt said. "I'm just going in mental circles here. Mind…shut up."

Minutes later blessed slumber claimed him.

The following four days and nights in Nanjing flew by as the new families formalized their adoptions. The pending issue of the visa for Caitlin's second baby rose to the fore again on the day the passport photographs were taken, but Elizabeth told her to stay calm, have pictures done of both girls and they'd tackle the visa situation when they arrived in Guangzhou.

Once the official business was taken care of for the day, they went on wonderful sightseeing trips, with the babies taking it all in stride. Everyone scurried to buy more and more film as they attempted to record everything they were experiencing.

Caitlin's adjustments in Madison and Mackenzie's formula resulted in the girls eagerly devouring their bottles with no tummyaches following. They woke once in the night to eat and Matt and Caitlin got up together and fed them, chatting quietly as they each held a hungry bundle about what they had seen and done that day.

It was memory-making fun. It was smiles and

laughter, sunny skies and perfect weather. It was buying so many souvenirs that Elizabeth made arrangements with the hotel to help the shoppers box up their purchases and mail them to their addresses in Ventura. It was people who had dreamed of being parents for so long glorying in their new roles, with Bud declaring that this father business was even better than he'd ever imagined it would be.

It was Caitlin and Matt spending endless hours together with the twins. And each night it became more and more difficult to leave the other and go to their own rooms, where they tossed and turned until sleep claimed them.

They all shared a delicious dinner at a fancy restaurant on the last night in Nanjing, raising their glasses in a toast to the fact that the adoptions were final, their daughters were officially theirs... forever.

The next day they flew to Guangzhou and checked into the White Swan Hotel, which was like something out of a fairy tale, complete with a towering waterfall that flowed from three stories up in the center of the enormous lobby.

The suite assigned to Caitlin and Matt was even larger than the one they'd shared in Nanjing. By unspoken agreement they left both cribs in the living room despite the fact that a crying baby woke her sister. Neither Caitlin nor Matt wished to give up the time they spent together in the middle of the night sitting and feeding the girls. Besides, Caitlin rationalized, it was easier to have the twins on the same schedule. Once she was home and tackling their care alone, she'd work out a system to assure that each of her daughters was held in equal allotments of time.

On the morning of the third day in Guangzhou, Elizabeth found Caitlin, Matt and the twins as they were emerging from the dining room after breakfast.

"Well, this is it," Elizabeth said. "We have an appointment with Brian Hudson, who issues the visas, in half an hour. We can walk from here and it takes about fifteen minutes. Do you want to go to your room and change the babies before we leave?"

Caitlin nodded. "Yes, and we'll bring along a bottle for each." She sighed. "Oh, I don't want to go. I've been burying my head in the sand, pretending the problem of the second visa doesn't exist. What if… No, I can't bear the thought. No."

"We'll figure out something," Elizabeth said, unable to produce a smile. "Hurry along now. I'll wait for you down here."

In the suite Caitlin and Matt changed the babbling babies' diapers, then Matt put them in their cribs while Caitlin packed some supplies in a tote bag. After dropping bibs three times before she could tuck them in the bag, she sank onto the sofa.

"I'm terrified, Matt," she said, struggling against threatening tears.

"Me, too. Come on, Caitlin, we have to go downstairs. We're in enough trouble without being late for the appointment."

"Could you do your sunshine thing?" she asked, looking up at him. "Tell me that everything is going to work out just fine, and I shouldn't worry, and every glass you ever met in your entire life was half-full?"

Matt chuckled. "No."

"Oh."

Brian Hudson was a portly gentlemen in his early sixties, who greeted Elizabeth with a hug and smiled warmly at Caitlin and Matt and the twins. His smile, however, was replaced by a deep frown as Elizabeth explained the situation surrounding Caitlin and the babies. He tossed his pen on the large desk he sat behind and leaned back in a worn and creaking leather chair.

"Elizabeth, you know I have no authority to issue a second visa. I can only document the number that the INS is aware of for your group. Caitlin was approved, as a single mother, to adopt one child. The INS felt she had the financial, physical and emotional ability to do that. But a single woman suddenly saying she's adopting two babies?''

Brian shook his head. ''She's not allowed to use any government-funded agencies for assistance or…'' He looked at the girls who were being held by Caitlin and Matt. ''They sure are cute, aren't they? The thought of separating them, leaving one behind is…I don't have a magic solution to pull out of a hat like a rabbit.''

''I can't leave one of my babies behind. I won't. They're my daughters and I love them, don't you understand? Oh, please, there has to be a way to solve this.''

''We're not getting on a plane without both of these babies,'' Matt said, narrowing his eyes.

''I'm not the bad guy here.'' Brian threw up his hands. ''These aren't *my* rules, but I have to follow them. If I did issue a visa without INS approval it wouldn't be valid.''

''But,'' Caitlin said.

''Everyone, calm down,'' Elizabeth said firmly. ''Now, Brian, listen to me. Remember five years ago when we discovered at the last minute that one of our couples in the group who had adopted a baby girl was told in a casual remark by a caregiver that their daughter had a four-year-old brother still at the orphanage who was blind?''

''Oh, yes.'' Brian chuckled. ''That was quite an experience once you got the bee in your bonnet to help those folks get that boy. I think we wore out our fax machine sending documents to the INS assuring them that the couple would finance all special training for the youngster, were emotionally prepared to deal with his handicap and... You were awesome in action, my friend.''

''And the INS allowed you to issue the second visa,'' Elizabeth said, leaning forward in her chair. ''My couple adopted both of those kids and they all flew home at the same time.''

''So they did,'' Brian said, nodding. ''Then I took a very long nap.'' He paused and narrowed his eyes. ''Okay, Elizabeth Kane, what sneaky little plan do you have up your sleeve *this* time?''

''Elizabeth?'' Caitlin asked, her heart starting to race.

Matt popped two antacid tablets in his mouth.

''All right,'' Elizabeth said. ''Caitlin's application to adopt one child as a single mother was approved months ago, months and months ago. But, you see, since then her circumstances have changed.''

''Is that a fact?'' Brian smiled and shook his head. ''And just what has occurred in Ms. Cunningham's life that would make her unquestionably eligible to be the mother of twins?''

Elizabeth beamed. ''Caitlin got married. She is now—ta-da—Mrs. Matt MacAllister.''

Chapter Ten

Brian Hudson, Caitlin thought, from what seemed like a faraway place, was wearing a very attractive tie. He no doubt knew where the best places were to shop in Guangzhou due to the fact that he lived here. Then again, maybe he had family in the United States and someone had sent him the tie for his birthday or...

She had gotten married and was now Mrs. Matt MacAllister?

"What?" Caitlin said in a squeaky little voice that she immediately decided couldn't be hers.

"Could you," Matt said, staring into space. "Could you run that by me again? I don't believe I heard you correctly."

"Everyone just stay calm," Elizabeth said, patting the air with flattened hands. "It's brilliant. It will work. Brian, you know as well as I do that the people at the INS who handle international adoptions are just as thrilled about these kids getting a chance at a decent life as we are. I know that because I've spoken to them personally."

Brian laced his fingers over his ample stomach and nodded, an expression of deep concentration on his face.

"They have to follow the rules and regs regarding paperwork," Elizabeth rushed on, "so we supply them with paperwork. You're authorized to marry people, so you perform the ceremony for Caitlin and Matt.

"Then you fax the INS a letter stating that you're simply updating Caitlin's file and informing them that she is no longer a single woman, because she has a husband. It isn't necessary to reveal how long she has had said husband.

"You also tell them that due to a glitch in Beijing, the fact that Caitlin—oh, and Matt—were matched with twins didn't come to light until we got here, but that's fine because they're a couple, wife and husband, mom and dad, and blah, blah, blah, and perfectly capable of taking care of the girls on all levels…physically, financially and emotionally."

Brian nodded. "It could work."

"It *would* work," Elizabeth said. "You request permission to issue another visa and we're home free. There. That's settled. My goodness, I amaze myself sometimes when my mighty mind kicks into action."

"Excuse me," Caitlin said, raising one finger. "This...um...wedding ceremony that Mr. Hudson would perform...is it legal and binding in the United States, or only official here in China?"

"Oh, it's for real everywhere," Elizabeth said. "Brian's status at the consulate gives him the power to do all kinds of nifty things. You and Matt can have the marriage quietly annulled once you return home, of course, but we're concentrating on getting that second visa and this is the way to do it.

"We're not breaking the law, we're just wiggling around it...sort of. The INS will be happy because they'll have the paperwork they need, and you get to take both girls with you when you leave." Elizabeth paused. "Matt? Any comments?"

"I'm just wondering if Bud would agree to be my best man."

Caitlin's head snapped around and her mouth dropped open for a moment as she stared at Matt. "That's what's on your mind?" she said, nearly shrieking. "Whether Bud will stand up with you? Matt, these people are talking about us getting married. As in…I do, and in sickness and health, and better or worse, until we croak and…'' She pressed one hand on her flushed forehead. ''I'm losing it. But, dear heaven, this is insane.''

''This,'' Matt said firmly, ''is the solution to our problem. Elizabeth, you are to be commended for coming up with this plan.''

''Thank you,'' she said, obviously pleased with herself. ''I admit that I'm rather proud of myself.''

''But,'' Caitlin said, then mentally threw up her hands.

''Having Marsha and Bud as your witnesses is fine,'' Elizabeth said, ''but we won't tell the rest of the group what has taken place. We're not breaking rules, we're just bending them, but the fewer people that know the better.''

''No problem,'' Matt said.

''But,'' Caitlin started again, then realized she was not capable of stringing words together to make a coherent sentence.

''Well,'' Brian said, getting to his feet, ''let's do the deed. You don't have that many days left here in Guangzhou, and we need that permission to issue another visa pronto. The sooner I can fax them the new data the better. I'll go get the forms needed so I can marry you folks.''

''Now?'' Caitlin said, jumping to her feet and startling Madison, who began to cry.

"The sooner the better," Brian said, then left the room.

"I'll call the hotel and see if Bud and Marsha are there," Elizabeth said, rising. "If they went sight-seeing we'll just have to settle for witnesses from the staff here. I'll go find a phone."

As Elizabeth hurried from the room, Caitlin soothed Madison, then placed her in a playpen that had been provided for the little ones. Matt laid Mackenzie on her tummy next to her sister. Caitlin sank back onto her chair as her trembling legs refused to hold her for another moment. She glared at Matt.

"Why are you so calm about this?"

Matt smiled. "My doctor told me that stress is bad for my health."

Caitlin leaned toward him. "Read my lips. You are getting married. Today. To me."

"Yep," he said, nodding. "That's what's happening, by golly. Elizabeth is something, isn't she? Think about it, Caitlin. We don't have to face the heartbreak of leaving one of the girls behind. God, I can't even imagine that scenario, I really can't. But Mackenzie and Madison are both going home. You should be smiling, not looking like the dentist just announced that you need six root canals."

"Yes," Caitlin said slowly. "Yes, of course, you're right. I was just so stunned by… But my focus should be on the babies, and the fact that everything is going to be fine, and Mr. Hudson will issue the visa and… We'll just cancel the marriage after we get back to Ventura. Sure. Okay.''

No, Matt thought suddenly. Cancel the marriage? Erase it? Pretend it never happened? Caitlin was certainly quick to get that laid out on the table. Hello, husband. Goodbye, husband. Thanks for your help. Have a nice life. Buzz off, MacAllister.

What if he didn't want to cancel the marriage, as Caitlin put it? He was…oh, God, he was in love with this woman, and he loved those babies, and once Brian did his thing they would be a family. An honest-to-goodness family. What if he didn't want to be erased?

Whoa, Matt thought, getting to his feet and beginning to pace. Where was his mind going? Yes, he loved Caitlin, had actually fallen in love with her. But marry her? Now? All that hearth-and-home stuff was for later when he figured out how to be the best in two arenas and…

But later, somewhere in the future, Caitlin might have married someone else, fallen in love and vowed to stay by that man's side until death parted them. Mackenzie and Madison would have a father who wouldn't be him.

Somewhere in the future he would still be alone and so damn lonely it sent chills down his spine just thinking about it.

Matt stopped his trek and looked at Caitlin, who

was staring at her hands that were clutched tightly in her lap.

He was going to marry the woman he loved, Matt thought. The timing was off from his master plan but so be it. He'd have some major adjustments to make in his work schedule, but he'd deal with that…somehow.

Matt frowned.

What he should be zeroing in on was the dismal fact that while he was about to marry the woman he loved, the woman he was about to marry didn't love him. She was already talking about canceling him out of her life before they'd even tied the knot. Just undo the knot and ship him off to Buffalo. Hell.

Matt shoved his hands in his pockets and resumed pacing.

Married, Caitlin thought, with a weary sigh. This should be such a happy day in her life, but the reality of the situation could not be ignored. The wedding ceremony that Brian Hudson would perform was a sham, a means to an end, which would guarantee that both of her daughters could go home to Ventura.

It was a marriage of convenience, per se, which was about as romantic as stale bread.

Focus, Caitlin, she ordered herself. She must concentrate on the purpose of this marriage, the fact that without it, she would be forced to leave one of her precious daughters behind when she left, and that was totally unacceptable.

She'd blank her mind during the necessary ceremony, repeat her lines by rote, knowing they meant nothing, not really. She could only hope that Brian Hudson whizzed through the exchanging of vows and got it over with as quickly as possible before she burst into depressed tears.

If she did think at all it would be about Mackenzie and Madison and the realization that she was doing this for them and for herself when she was wearing her mother hat. It had absolutely nothing to do with her woman hat. Nothing.

Caitlin's tormented thoughts were interrupted by Elizabeth and Brian reentering the room followed by a breathless Marsha and Bud. Caitlin got to her feet and was immediately hugged by a beaming Marsha.

"Isn't this exciting?" Marsha said. "It's awesome, it's wonderful, it's—"

"It doesn't mean a thing. This wedding ceremony, Matt and I getting married, is for the single purpose of making it possible to get the second visa, Marsha. It's a temporary situation that will be undone…for lack of a better word…once we return to Ventura."

Marsha grabbed Caitlin's arm and hauled her to the end of the room. "But you and Matt care for each other," Marsha said, her voice hushed. "More than care, from what I've witnessed going on between the two of you. Personally I think you two are in love with each other.''

"Don't be silly,'' Caitlin said, averting her gaze from Marsha's. ''We haven't even known each other very long.''

"What difference does that make? When you meet your soul mate—blam—that's it. When you two are together there is so much…something… crackling through the air between you it's a wonder there aren't visible flames dancing around.''

"Lust is not love,'' Caitlin said, lifting her chin. ''You're misinterpreting what you're seeing. I care for Matt. I'll admit that. But I would never marry a man who is as dedicated to his career as he is, no matter how I felt about him. Which is not to say that how I feel about him is of any great significance at this point in time. Am I making myself clear?''

"Honey, you and Matt have been making yourselves clear from the get-go.''

"Darn it, Marsha, I—''

"Are we ready to proceed?'' Brian said.

No, Caitlin thought.

"Yes,'' she said.

Elizabeth peered into the playpen. ''The kiddies are going to miss the whole shebang. They're sound asleep.''

"Rings," Bud said. "I'm the best man. I'm supposed to hand Matt a ring to put on Caitlin's finger."

Caitlin crossed the room with Marsha right behind her.

"Forget about rings, Bud," Caitlin said. "This is not a wedding in the normal sense of the word. Right, Matt?"

Matt didn't answer for so long that Caitlin looked at him questioningly.

"Matt?"

"Oh. Right. This is a marriage—"

"Of convenience, to use a Victorian term. We say 'I do' so Mr. Hudson can say, 'I do hereby issue a second visa.' End of story."

"I don't think so," Marsha said in a singsong voice.

Caitlin glared at her, then directed her attention to Brian.

"Shall we proceed?" she said. Before she started to cry and couldn't stop, because she was hating this, really hating this. "Please?"

"Certainly," Brian said.

Everyone took their places and Brian opened a book, flipping through the pages.

"Okay, here it is," he said. "We are gathered here today to unite this man and this woman in holy matrimony. Do you, Matt, take Caitlin to be your lawfully wedded wife, to love her, cherish her, through…''

Caitlin forced herself to tune out what Brian was saying as tears misted her eyes.

She couldn't do this, she thought frantically. Yes, she could. She had to.

''I do,'' Matt said, his voice ringing with conviction that caused everyone in the room to stare at him.

''Thought so,'' Marsha said.

''Do you, Caitlin,'' Brian went on, ''take Matt to be your…''

Two tears slid down Caitlin's pale cheeks and Elizabeth pressed a tissue into Caitlin's hand. Matt encircled her shoulders with one arm and eased her close to his side.

''Caitlin?'' Brian said.

''What?'' she said, dabbing at her nose. ''Oh. Yes. I do.''

''By the power invested in me,'' Brian boomed, ''I now pronounce you husband and wife.''

Forever, Matt thought fiercely. There were a million hurdles blocking the path to that forever but somehow, somehow, he'd plow them down, one by one. He was in love with Caitlin and she was now his wife. Oh, man, that sounded so terrific. And he was Mackenzie and Madison's daddy and… He was about to begin a battle for his future happiness, for his very life...with Caitlin. The war was on and he intended to win...somehow.

"Temporary wife," Caitlin said.

"Shh," Matt said. "That's not written in the book."

"You may kiss the bride," Brian said.

"Oh, well, that isn't necessary," Caitlin said, "because..."

Matt framed Caitlin's face with his hands, then claimed her mouth in a kiss that was so soft, so gentle, so reverent that fresh tears spilled onto her cheeks.

"Oh-h-h," Marsha said. "I just love weddings." She sniffled. "This is so romantic, so... Oh-h-h."

Matt lifted his head and smiled at Caitlin.

"Hello, Mrs. MacAllister," he said.

The sudden sound of a crying baby saved Caitlin from having to respond to her new title.

"That's Madison," she and Matt said in unison.

"Well, well, well," Elizabeth said, "we know which baby is crying without looking, do we? That's a true sign of a dedicated mommy and daddy. I'd bet that you both can tell them apart by now, too, without looking for the fingernail polish on tiny toes."

"Sure can," Matt said.

"Are we finished here?" Caitlin said, her voice quivering.

"There are papers to sign," Brian said. "Caitlin,

since the adoption documents show the twins with the last name of Cunningham, sign the marriage certificate as Caitlin Cunningham. The INS won't blink an eye at that. They'll just assume you're an eccentric couple who gave the babies their mother's name and the mother kept her name and…whatever. My cover letter will assure them that you all are, indeed, the MacAllister family.''

Amen, Matt thought. Forever.

For now, Caitlin thought miserably. Only for a tick of time.

In a foggy blur, Caitlin signed her name where Brian indicated, then went to the playpen and lifted a still-crying Madison into her arms. Mackenzie slept on.

''Marsha, Bud,'' Matt said after signing the documents, ''are you going back to the hotel? Can you help Caitlin with the babies? I have something I need to do.''

''Sure,'' Marsha said. ''We left Grace with Jane and Bill because our sweetie was due to eat, then sleep. We can tote as many babies as need toting.''

''We only have two,'' Matt said, laughing. ''Which is quite enough…for now.''

''For now?'' Marsha raised her eyebrows.

''Figure of speech, I'm sure,'' Caitlin said quickly. ''Mr. Hudson, I can't begin to thank you for all you're doing to assure that the twins will be able to stay together. I hope you know how grateful—''

''We are,'' Matt interjected, reaching out and pumping Brian's hand. ''On behalf of all members of the newly created MacAllister family I sincerely thank you, sir.''

''My pleasure. Elizabeth, I'll be in touch and keep you informed as to how we're doing with the flurry of faxes that is about to start between here and the INS in the States. The minute I receive permission to issue that second visa I'll call you at the hotel.''

''Splendid,'' Elizabeth said, then kissed Brian on the cheek. ''You're a dear for doing this.''

''No, I just know better than to argue with you when you get a bee in your bonnet, Elizabeth. Well, best of luck to all of you.''

''I'm gone,'' Matt said. ''I'll see you back at the hotel, Mrs. MacAllister.'' He strode from the room.

''Stop calling me that,'' Caitlin said, shaking her head.

''Why?'' Marsha said, taking Madison from Caitlin's arms. ''That's who you are now, Caitlin.''

''She's also exhausted,'' Bud said. ''That's the doctor part of me talking. Caitlin, you are stressed to the max. I hereby prescribe a nap for you. Marsha and I will tend to your girls for the next two hours. You are to march yourself back to the hotel and stretch out on the bed.''

"Oh, but—"

"Go," Bud said, pointing to the door.

"Thank you," Caitlin said, her shoulders slumping with fatigue. "I feel as though I need to concentrate just to put one foot in front of the other." She glanced around the room. "This was quite an experience. I—" A soft cry interrupted her. "Mackenzie is awake."

"I'll get her," Bud said. "Ah, there's the tote bag with all the treasures needed to keep little ladies fed and dry. Goodbye, Caitlin."

"Thank you. I'm sure I'll be as good as new after I rest a bit. I don't know why I'm so exhausted, so drained."

"Well, it's not every day that a person gets married, you know," Marsha said, then cringed when she saw Caitlin's stricken expression. "Forget I said that. Go take a nap."

With one last long look at Mackenzie and Madison, Caitlin left the room, then the building. She walked slowly along the tree-lined sidewalk, oblivious to the people around her and the usual battle of bicycles versus cars taking place on the road.

Oh, my, she thought. She was doing her half-and-half thing again. Part of her was so thankful, so relieved that a solution had been found regarding the second visa.

But it was that very solution that was causing her to feel so...so sad. A woman's wedding day, the ceremony where sacred vows were exchanged with the man of her heart, a pledge made to stand side by side until death parted them, should be one of the happiest days of her life.

But she was miserable.

Her marriage to Matt was nothing more than a charade. That was about the crummiest wedding day imaginable.

Focus on Mackenzie and Madison, Caitlin told herself over and over like a mantra.

When she finally reached the hotel suite, she slipped off her shoes and stretched out on the bed in her room.

She wished she could pour out her tale of woe to her mother, Caitlin thought, but that wouldn't be fair because her mother was worried enough about Paulo's health without having a weeping daughter calling long distance.

No, she'd share the news of the twins after returning safely to Ventura. Maybe she'd never tell her mother about having been Matt's wife to accomplish the goal of obtaining the second visa. What was the point of sharing that newsflash when the marriage would be over as quickly as the paperwork could be completed?

Her mother didn't need to know that along with coming home from China with two beautiful daughters instead of one, she'd also arrived back in Ventura with a heart that was struggling frantically not to fall in love with the wrong man, a man who would shatter that heart into a million pieces that could never be put back together again.

Chapter Eleven

When Matt returned to the hotel he found a note from Bud and Marsha taped to the door of the suite. They were going on a sight-seeing tour, they said, and with the help of others in the group were taking Mackenzie and Madison along for the fun. They would probably be gone longer than the originally planned two hours, and Caitlin and Matt were not to worry about the twins.

"Bless you," Matt said, removing the paper. "I need all the time I can get for this."

He entered the suite, then frowned when he saw that Caitlin was not in the living room. He went to the open doorway of her bedroom and stopped, his gaze riveted on Caitlin where she lay sleeping. He set the bag he was carrying on a chair and went to the side of the bed, drinking in the sight of...

''My wife,'' he whispered.

And, oh, God, how he loved her.

While he'd been wandering the streets of Guangzhou after leaving the consulate, he'd realized that people were staring at the tall American who was striding along the sidewalk grinning like an idiot.

But he couldn't help smiling as the sense of pure joy, of being complete, whole, overflowed to show itself on his face. He was married to the woman he loved, the only woman he had ever, would ever love.

So, okay, maybe she didn't love him...not yet. But the kernel of caring was there within Caitlin, he just knew it was. If she'd give it a chance to grow, blossom into the wondrous love he felt for her, they could have a together together with their fantastic little girls.

Ah, Caitlin, Matt thought, still gazing at her. Give me a chance. Give *us* a chance. Please, my love.

As if sensing his presence, Caitlin stirred, then opened her eyes. Still foggy from her deep sleep, she registered only the fact that Matt was there. The man she must *not* fall in love with but who was, just for now, her husband.

''Hi,'' Matt said quietly. ''Marsha and Bud took

the twins on a sight-seeing tour. I need to talk to you, Caitlin. Are you awake enough to listen to what I have to say?''

Caitlin stared at Matt for a moment. ''All I know right now,'' she finally said, her voice slightly husky with sleep, ''is that this is our wedding day. This is another one of those stolen times apart from reality.'' She lifted her arms toward Matt. ''Just say it once more, Matt. Call me Mrs. MacAllister, then make love to me, your wife.''

''But I want to tell you that I—''

''Shh. No. Just say, 'Hello, Mrs. MacAllister.'''

A bolt of heated desire rocketed through Matt and the heartfelt words, the declaration of his love that he wanted Caitlin to hear floated into oblivion as his want of her consumed him.

As she slid off the bed to stand before him and remove her clothes, he tore at his own, tossing them to the floor, then reaching for her eagerly because she was just too far away.

They tumbled onto the bed, their lips meeting in a searing kiss. Matt finally raised his head to look directly into Caitlin's eyes.

''Hello, Mrs. MacAllister,'' he said, his voice gritty with passion.

''Hello, Mr. MacAllister,'' she whispered.

Matt felt as though his heart would burst with love as he kissed her again, gently this time, with a sense of awe and wonder at how quickly and intensely he'd fallen in love with this exquisite woman. His wife.

His wife, his mind sang, as though a chorus of angels was announcing it to the world.

They'd made love before, but this, he knew, was special and new, the consummating of their marriage, the sealing of the bond, the commitment to forever as husband and wife.

Caitlin loved him, *she did,* because she had wanted to hear him say, "Hello, Mrs. MacAllister," have those words entwine with her reply of "Hello, Mr. MacAllister," words that warmed his heart, his mind, his very soul.

Caitlin sank her fingers into Matt's thick hair and urged his mouth to claim hers once again.

They kissed and caressed, hands never still, lips and tongues tasting and savoring, hearts racing and breathing becoming labored.

Matt raised above Caitlin, then filled her with all that he was as a man and she received him with all that she was as a woman. The perfectly synchronized tempo of their rocking bodies was wild and earthy. They clung tightly to each other as they were carried up and away, then were flung into the brightly colored place they had yearned to go to.

It was ecstasy. It was so beautiful it defied description in its splendor.

Hello, Mr. and Mrs. MacAllister.

Matt collapsed against Caitlin, his energy spent,

then mustered enough strength to move off her. He tucked her close to his side. They were silent as their bodies cooled and hearts quieted.

"Caitlin," Matt said finally, breaking the dreamy silence in the room, "will you listen to me now? I want, I need, to tell you something."

"Mmm. Yes. All right."

Matt shifted just enough to enable him to look directly into Caitlin's eyes that still held the lingering smoky hue of desire. "I...Caitlin, I love you. I've fallen deeply and forever in love with you. And I love Mackenzie and Madison and...I believe, I hope and pray, that you love me, too."

"No, don't say that you love me." Tears filled her eyes. "It's difficult enough for me to... No."

"Caitlin, I know that you care for me, may even be in love with me although you won't admit it," he said, his voice raspy with emotion. "Everything could be perfect. Just perfect. We're already married. We're husband and wife and the parents of the two most fantastic babies in the world.

"I want to spend the rest of my life coming in the door at night and saying, 'Hello, Mrs. Mac-Allister.' We'll be a family, the four of us. Ah, Caitlin, I love you so much. I'm a husband, a father, you're my wife and—"

"No." Caitlin pressed her hands on Matt's chest to gain her freedom from his embrace, then left the bed and began to gather her clothes. "No."

Matt sat up and stared at her. "Why? Why are you doing this? We both love our daughters and—"

"They're *my* daughters," she said, clutching her clothes and ignoring the tears that spilled onto her cheeks. "It doesn't matter what my feelings for you might or might not be. This marriage will be over just as soon as the proper steps can be taken to end it when we return to Ventura."

Matt stood and gripped Caitlin's bare shoulders. "Why won't you give us a chance to have a future together?"

"Because you're him," she yelled. "You're him. You're just like my father, Matt. Your career comes first to the point that nothing else matters. Oh, yes, you'd be so sorry that you missed the twins' birthday party, or didn't get home in time to keep the reservation at the restaurant where we were going to dinner to celebrate our anniversary. So very sorry.

"But you'd do it again and again and again. Always so sorry, but telling me, telling the girls that we should be able to understand that what you do for a living is vitally important and… No. I made a vow years ago that I would never marry a man who was centered on his work, had tunnel vision about his career.

"And then here you were, attempting to steal my heart. But I won't be your wife and you won't be the father to Mackenzie and Madison. I won't re-live the heartache I grew up with, saw my mother suffer through, nor will I subject my daughters to it. *My daughters.* They're mine, Matt, and I'm going to protect my heart and theirs from you.''

''No, no,'' Matt said, a frantic edge to his voice. ''I'll change. I have no intention of putting in the kind of hours I did before at the hospital. I'll delegate and…I swear to you that my focus will be on you and the babies, us, our family. I *will* change, Caitlin, I promise you that.''

Caitlin closed her eyes for a moment and her shoulders slumped with fatigue and defeat.

''No, you won't change,'' she said, hardly above a whisper. ''Oh, I believe you intend to, actually believe you're capable of doing that, but I know better.''

''Damn it, Caitlin,'' Matt said, dragging a restless hand through his hair. ''I am not your father.''

''No, you're not,'' she said. ''Nor will you be Mackenzie and Madison's father, or my husband. I can't live in the world you would bring to our lives. I can't. I won't.''

''Don't do this to me, to us, to the twins,'' Matt said, holding out one hand toward her. ''Ah, please, Caitlin, give me a chance to prove to you that I—''

''No, no, no.''

''Don't do this,'' Matt said, his voice choked with emotion.

"I have to."

Caitlin turned and walked into the bathroom, closed the door, then seconds later the sound of water running in the shower could be heard.

Matt splayed one hand on his chest.

His heart hurt, he thought. It had nothing to do with his blood pressure or any of the other things that Bud had jumped on his case about. It was an emotional pain that was spreading, he could feel it consuming him, gripping his mind, his soul, in an icy fist.

Damn it, this wasn't fair. He was being judged and found guilty because of the sins of her father. Well, he wasn't her lousy dad, he was Matt MacAllister who...

Matt MacAllister who had pushed himself so hard executing his chosen career he'd nearly blown his health beyond repair. But, by damn, he had to be the best at what he did, have a flag to wave just like all the other MacAllisters.

But he understood that now. He'd been wrong. It had taken Caitlin to make him realize that. Caitlin and those babies. He was going to change. When they returned to Ventura, Caitlin would see that his promise was going to be kept. She'd see.

Oh, really? a nasty, niggling voice whispered in Matt's mind. How was she going to *see* when she had no intention of letting him come near her when they were home?

"I'll figure that out later," Matt said, beginning to gather his clothes.

Caitlin emerged from the bathroom in the clothes she'd been wearing earlier. "You'd better shower and dress," she said, not looking at him. "We don't know for certain when Marsha and Bud are going to bring the babies back, so..."

"Yeah, okay." Matt scooped up the last article of clothing from the floor. He straightened and looked over at Caitlin, who was smoothing the bed linens. "I love you, Caitlin. I want to spend the rest of my life with you, with our babies. And you love me, or at least you're damn close to it. This isn't over yet, not by a long shot."

Matt waited for her to reply, then when she didn't he went into the bathroom and closed the door.

"Yes, it *is* over, Matt," Caitlin said to the empty room, covering her face with her trembling hands. "It is."

When Matt came into the living room, having showered and dressed in clean clothes, he found Caitlin sitting on the sofa, flipping through a magazine. He went into her bedroom and returned with the bag he'd placed on the chair.

"Caitlin?" he said, standing in front of her.

"Hmm?"

"I went shopping when I left the consulate," he said quietly. "I got this."

Caitlin raised her head slowly, then her breath caught when she saw Matt take a tiny red dress from the bag.

"I didn't think it was right that one of the girls would have a red dress for the farewell dinner," he went on, leaning forward and placing the dress on her lap. "So, I... Then I saw this..." He drew a bundle of silk from the bag. "It's for you to wear that night. It's white but it has red flowers down the front. See? You'll be wearing red, too, and I bought myself a bright red tie. I pictured us all in my mind in our red finery, the MacAllister family." He put the blouse on top of the red dress.

"Oh, Matt," Caitlin said, shaking her head as fresh tears threatened. "This...all of this is so sweet, so thoughtful and..."

"Will you wear the blouse that night?"

"Yes, of course I will. Thank you. And thank you for buying the second red dress. I forgot all about the fact that I only have one with me and... You're a very—"

"Dedicated father," he said, a slight edge to his voice, "but I don't get any lasting points for that, do I?"

"Matt, don't. Please...just don't."

"Yes, ma'am," he said, saluting her. "Whatever you say, ma'am. After all, you're obviously running this show. You put me on trial, found me guilty, sentenced me to a future without you, without my daughters, without giving me an opportunity to defend myself, prove to you that I—

"Hell, forget it. You're not hearing what I'm saying. You've made up your mind about me. I'm a carbon copy of your father. Case closed." He paused. "I'll be in my bedroom practicing smiling until Marsha and Bud bring the girls back."

Matt strode into his bedroom, closed the door, then sank onto the edge of the bed. He reached into the bag he was still holding and took out a small box covered in flocked red satin. He opened it, then stared at what was inside through tear-filled eyes.

Wedding rings, he thought. Matching. Gold. With Chinese lettering that said love and happiness. Shiny rings that represented a bright future for a man and woman who planned to be together as husband and wife. Forever.

Matt snapped the box closed, the sound seeming to strike him like a physical blow that caused a moan to rumble in his chest. He looked at the box, the trash can next to the bed, then back at the box.

No, damn it, he thought fiercely. He wasn't throwing these rings away. They represented his future with Caitlin. He wasn't giving up on what he knew in his mind, his heart and soul, that they could have together.

He was going to fight for it, for her, for their daughters, with every breath in his body.

Chapter Twelve

Caitlin sighed as the airplane gained altitude and the last glimpse of the land below was covered by a marshmallow cloud. She sank back in her seat.

"I'm eager to return home," she said, "but I hate to leave China, too. It's so beautiful and intriguing and I'll never see it again."

Wrong, Matt thought. He'd already decided that a trip back to this country was in order when the twins were teenagers so they could learn more about their heritage, their roots. They'd all come, the MacAllister family, including the children he and Caitlin had created together. Yep, that was on his mental agenda.

"It's a nice place, but I wouldn't want to live there," he said pleasantly. "I'm looking forward to drinks with ice in the glass, mayonnaise on my sandwiches, and eating a meal that doesn't include a fried egg. Besides, I'll never master using chopsticks. Ventura, here I come."

Matt leaned forward and peered in the bassinets that were mounted on the bulkhead in front of them.

"How about you two Miss M.'s?" he said, switching his gaze back and forth between the twins. "Ready to become California surfers?"

The babies kicked their feet and waved tiny fists in the air.

"Right on," Matt said. "You're learning how to do high fives like pros." He chuckled, settled back in his seat again and took a magazine from the side pocket.

Caitlin slid a glance at Matt from beneath her lashes, then looked out the window of the plane again as though fluffy white stuff was the most fascinating thing she had ever seen.

She did not, she thought, understand Matt MacAllister, not even close. After the emotional scene in the hotel suite when she'd said that she would not, could not, marry him, she fully expected him to brood, be angry, hurt, whatever. She was dreading the remainder of the stay in Guangzhou as she anticipated an ever-growing tension between them.

But none of that had taken place.

When Marsha and Bud had returned the twins to the suite, Matt had been cheerful and smiling and hadn't dropped his life-is-grand facade since.

They'd gone on sight-seeing tours with the others, shopped in a quaint marketplace and continued to take endless photographs.

The wonderful news had been delivered by Elizabeth that the INS had approved the issuing of the second visa and off they'd gone to the consulate to meet with a beaming Brian.

They'd dressed in their red finery for the farewell dinner the previous night, with Matt insisting that Bud take several pictures of Matt, her and the twins together.

Oh, yes, Matt was acting very weird, Caitlin mentally rambled on. How could a man who had declared his love to a woman, proposed to her, been turned down flat, be so darn happy?

Was Matt slipping back into his old, the-glass-is-half-full demeanor that had been in place when she'd met him? No, she didn't think so. The way he was behaving now was different in an unexplainable way. It was unsettling, to say the least, and her nerves were shot.

She was sad, too. She refused to look deep within herself to determine if she was in love with

Matt because it was so hopeless. She had to some-how, *somehow,* get on with her life with the twins without Matt, never see him again, and if anyone looked at her crooked she'd burst into tears.

"Caitlin?" Matt said, bringing her from her gloomy thoughts.

"What," she said much too loudly.

"Jeez, did I wake you?"

"No, I'm sorry. I didn't mean to bark at you. What did you want to say?"

Matt shrugged. "I was just going to chat, com-ment on the fact that Elizabeth has covered every detail by having Carolyn bring an extra baby car seat to the airport so we can transport these little critters home." He paused. "You're short one crib, though."

"Well, I'll worry about that later. The girls are small enough to both fit in the one crib until I can get another one."

"Try this. I'm still on leave from the hospital, you know. Why don't I go to the store the day after we get back and buy another crib to match the one we bought. I'll bring it over and put it together for you."

"Oh, no, I don't think—"

"Do you have a better plan?"

"Well, no," Caitlin said, "but—"

"That settles it then. I'll get some more diapers, too. What else do you think you'll need? Food for yourself? Well, sure, that makes sense. You must have cleaned out your refrigerator before leaving for so long. While we're on this flight, start making a list that lasts thirty-two days and I'll grocery shop for you.''

''Why are you doing this?'' Caitlin said, leaning toward him.

''Doing what?'' he said, an expression of pure innocence on his face.

''Being so...so nice to me.''

''I happen to be a nice person, Ms. Cunningham,'' Matt said.

''You're a confusing person,'' Caitlin said, slouching back in her seat again.

Matt faked a cough to cover the burst of laughter that escaped from his throat.

Caitlin was rattled, he thought smugly. Big-time. And he was exhausted. It was taking every bit of his acting ability, such as it was, to present the appearance that he was doing just fine, thank you very much.

But he wasn't.

He had a cold fist in his gut that refused to go away, a chilling dread that no matter how hard he tried, no matter how hard he fought to prove to Caitlin that he would be a dedicated husband and father, she wouldn't believe it. He would fail.

He was going to change his lifestyle, and he'd figure out ways to be certain that she *did* see that it was happening. He couldn't lose her. He couldn't lose his family. His future. His everything. No.

Caitlin yawned and Matt looked at her and frowned.

"You're tired," he said. "Why don't you snooze for a while?"

"Not while the babies are awake. They might decide they want a bottle or a dry diaper."

"Which I am perfectly capable of tending to. You have the little pillow and the blanket that were on our seats. You can curl up and use the middle seat here, plus yours." He patted his right thigh. "You can plop your pillow on my leg if you want to and have even more room."

No way, Caitlin thought. She wasn't about to snuggle up to Matt like that. No, no, no.

"If you're certain you don't mind if I take a nap. I will."

Matt patted his thigh again. "Go for it."

Caitlin propped the pillow on the upper part of her seat next to the window, turned her back on Matt and curled up into a ball.

"Nudge me if you need help with the twins," she said, her voice muffled.

That, Matt thought, staring at Caitlin's back, had *not* gone well.

He sighed, folded his arms on his chest and glowered into space. He had to hang in there, not give up, just keep chipping away at Caitlin's defensive wall until it crumbled into dust.

Caitlin stirred, opened her eyes and wondered foggily why her nose was smushed into a lumpy, minuscule pillow. Realizing where she was as the last of the misty curtain of sleep dissipated, she unfolded her legs and cringed as she stretched her stiff muscles. She turned her head and her eyes widened.

Matt was feeding Mackenzie a bottle while she lay on his thighs, and had another bottle poked into Madison's mouth where she was tucked next to him on her back in the vacant seat separating Caitlin from him.

"You're feeding them both at once? Why didn't you wake me? Why didn't I hear them crying?" She glanced at her watch. "I slept for two hours? What kind of mother sleeps through the wailing of her babies when they're hungry?"

"They didn't wail. They fussed, complained a bit, so I made up two bottles, asked the flight attendant to warm them, and here we are, doing fine."

"Well, I'm awake now so I'll finish feeding Madison."

"There's no need to disturb her. They're both about to drain the last drop and they're starting to doze already. They need to catch up on their sleep, too, after the big party last night at the hotel. We put them down for the night later than usual, you know.''

"They must need dry diapers.''

"I changed them while the bottles were being warmed.''

"Oh. Well. You certainly have everything under control, Matt.'' Caitlin laughed. "I feel like a fifth wheel, or a fourth wheel in this case.

"That's a very clever way to feed both of them, too. I figured I'd have to take turns propping one of their bottles, but I think you have a sixth sense when dealing with the babies. You're a natural-born father. I'll probably end up keeping my mothering manual close at hand when I get the girls home.''

"No, you won't,'' Matt said, easing the bottles out of the twins' mouths. "I've been there with you for many hours as we cared for these guys. Your instincts are right on target, Caitlin.''

"You're forgetting about the tummyache episode.''

"Believe me, I have not forgotten about the special delivery made to my bare chest the night of the tummies.'' He chuckled. "That will be a great story for me to tell them when they're older. They'll love hearing how Dad got plastered with formula when....'' Matt's voice trailed off and he looked at Caitlin.

A chill coursed through Matt as the menacing voice in his mind tormented him with the message that he might not be a part of the twins' lives when they were old enough to recognize the humor in the events of what would, by then, be a long-ago night.

"Ah, Caitlin, I..." He shook his head and stared at Mackenzie, who was sleeping peacefully.

It took all the willpower that Caitlin possessed to keep from reaching out and placing her hand on Matt's shoulder, telling him that she was certain the girls would enjoy the funny story he would relate to them at some point in the future.

She'd heard the anguish in his voice when he said, "Ah, Caitlin," saw it on his face and in the depths of his dark brown eyes. She wanted to erase his pain, push it into oblivion where it couldn't reach him.

But she couldn't do that, Caitlin thought, because there was no future for them. And *that* pain was hers to bear. They were in the countdown of hours now as they flew in the direction that would take them back to Ventura.

Ventura, California, where she would raise her daughters...alone.

The flight seemed endless.

All the babies in the group appeared to somehow sense that they were being held captive in that metal capsule and became cranky. Marsha and Bud took turns walking up and down the aisles with a whining Grace, ·and unhappy wails erupted from various parts of the airplane.

Caitlin told Matt that she felt sorry for the passengers who were not connected to them and were no doubt not pleased to have their attempts to sleep interrupted by a crying baby.

"No joke," Matt said. "I think I'd tell the flight attendant to stop and let me off of this flying day-care center. You and I aren't in a position to complain because Mackenzie and Madison are adding their two cents' worth to the racket. Oh, well, there are only about four more hours to go."

Caitlin looked at her watch. "Yes. Four hours."

And then? she thought. Oh, Caitlin, don't go there. She was torturing herself with the image in her mind of Matt driving her and the babies home from the airport, then leaving them in her cozy house, turning his back and walking away.

Granted, she would see him when he brought the second crib and put it together. But once that chore was done, he would leave again. Probably for the last time.

Mackenzie began to cry, and Caitlin scooped her out of the bassinet. "I'll walk with her for a bit."

Matt stood to allow Caitlin to reach the aisle, then sank back onto his seat. As if aware that her sister was receiving attention that she wasn't getting, Madison cut loose with an ear-splitting wail.

Matt lifted her from the bassinet and plopped her on his lap, facing him. "And what is the nature of your complaint, madam?" he said.

Madison stopped crying as suddenly as she had started and smiled at Matt.

"Spoiled rotten to the core," he said, laughing. "You ladies sure learn how to push a guy's buttons at a very early age." He looked up and his smile faded as he saw Caitlin in the distance. "But I love you anyway."

When the captain announced that they were beginning their descent into Ventura, Caitlin stiffened for a moment, then snapped on her seat belt as instructed. They would arrive at approximately 3:00 p.m. California time, the captain went on to say, and the weather was warm with a slight breeze.

"Home," Caitlin said. "I remember that I could hardly believe it when we were told we were about to land in Hong Kong, and now I'm having as much difficulty believing we're back in California." She paused. "I feel like I should say something profound like this is the first day of the rest of my life as a single mother of twins."

"Mmm," Matt said, frowning.

"Never mind." Caitlin waved one hand in the air. "I'm so tired I don't think I'm up for profound.

Did the captain say what day of the week it is? Crossing the international dateline certainly is confusing. I…ignore me, I'm blithering.''

''Are you nervous about tending to the twins on your own?'' Matt said quietly, looking over at Caitlin.

''Yes, I am,'' she said, meeting his gaze. ''But one of the first things I'm going to do is to call my mother and tell her that surprise, surprise, I came home from China with two daughters instead of one. My mother said not to call until I was back in Ventura so she could picture me with the baby in our home. I thought that was so sweet. I'm also hoping she has good news to share about Paulo.''

''Especially because she was so unhappy while married to your father. Right?'' Matt said.

Caitlin nodded.

''Don't you think you deserve happiness like that, too?'' he said.

''It's not that easy to find, Matt. Maybe it's there for me years from now. I'll meet a man who is retired, isn't focused on a demanding career and… Oh, I don't know. I'm just going to concentrate on being a mommy.''

''Caitlin, I love you,'' Matt said, his voice hushed so no one else could hear him, ''and I believe that you love me. If you'd just give us a chance, give *me* a chance to prove to you that I'm going to change and—''

"Don't," she said, shaking her head. "There is no point in getting into all that again, Matt. What happened between us belongs to the memories of China. All my physical and emotional energies must be focused on Mackenzie and Madison now."

Matt sank back in his seat and sighed. "Right."

When the airplane bumped onto the runway a cheer went up from the passengers and several babies began to cry.

"Ready?" Caitlin asked, looking at Matt as the plane door was opened and the people around them began collecting their belongings.

"Yep," he said, feeling that cold fist in his gut tighten even more. "Grab a kid, I'll take the other one, and let's get off of this machine."

As they made their way up the tunnel leading to the arrivals area in the airport, Caitlin frowned. "Look up ahead there. Am I just punchy exhausted or are there very bright lights by the doorway?"

"I don't know," Matt said, attempting to quiet a fussing Mackenzie who was squirming in his arms.

The bright lights were not a figment of Caitlin's imagination. They emerged from the tunnel to find a camera crew filming and an attractive woman with a microphone approaching the people with babies and speaking to them.

"What's all this?" Caitlin said as Madison started to cry. "Shh, sweetheart. It's okay."

"Matt MacAllister?" the woman with the microphone said, stepping in front of him. "This is an extra bonus for my story for the six o'clock news about these babies being adopted and brought here to Ventura. People know who you are and... Terrific.

"But, you son of a gun, I've interviewed you so many times regarding news at Mercy Hospital and you never mentioned that you were married. And now you're a daddy?" She looked quickly at Mackenzie and Madison. "Of twins? Fantastic. Why didn't you tell me you had a wife and that you planned to go to China and—"

"You never asked about my personal life, Sophie," Matt said, with a shrug. "But we're exhausted, the babies are getting hungry and—"

"Just a little footage," Sophie said. "Jerry, bring the camera and lights over here."

Caitlin said, "Oh, I don't think—"

"I'll make it quick," Sophie interrupted, then turned to face the camera. "And here is a familiar face to those who live in Ventura. Matt MacAllister, the highly respected public-relations director of Mercy Hospital.

"When we got the call from one of the new grandparents waiting for this group telling us that they were arriving today, we didn't know that Matt

MacAllister and his wife were among those bringing a baby home. In this case, two babies. Identical twins. Matt, your daughters are darling. How does it feel to be the father of twins?''

"I've enjoyed my role of daddy to these girls while we were in China."

"I bet you did," Sophie said, beaming. "Would you introduce your wife to our audience?"

"This is the mother of the twins. Caitlin."

"And how do you feel about your bundles of joy?" Sophie said, pushing the microphone in front of Caitlin's face.

"I'm...I'm thrilled," Caitlin said.

"Is Matt a helpful daddy?"

"He has been totally involved in their care."

"Matt, when did you get married and why did you keep it such a secret? Plus, why didn't you let us know you were making this momentous trip?"

Mackenzie had had enough of this nonsense and began to wail at top volume as she stiffened in Matt's arms.

"Sorry, Sophie," Matt said, edging around her, "but these babies need to eat and be put to bed without the sound of airplane engines roaring in their ears. Good to see you. Bye."

Matt strode away with Caitlin scrambling to reach his side again.

"Why did you do that?" she said, glancing quickly around to be certain no one was listening.

''She thinks we're married and you didn't set her straight.''

''Caitlin, I wasn't about to put our personal business on the six o'clock news. And if you think back over what I said, and how I phrased it, I never said that we are married. I'm a PR man, remember? I think very fast on my feet. Sophie assumed that we were married but I did *not* confirm that fact.''

Caitlin frowned. ''Oh. No, I guess you didn't, did you?''

''No. Hey, Carolyn, come meet Mackenzie and Madison.''

Carolyn hurried toward them carrying a car seat. ''Oh, they are so beautiful. Congratulations, Caitlin. Your daughters are exquisite. All the babies are gorgeous, aren't they? I love meeting these planes when they arrive. But you two look like what I'm used to seeing. Exhausted. Go. Shoo. Get those girls home so you can put your feet up. Remember what we told you, though, you should stay up as late as possible this evening to take care of your jet lag as quickly as it can be done.''

In a flurry of activity, Caitlin nestled Madison into the car seat, then they headed for the baggage-claim area, seeing several of the people from their group already going that way at a brisk clip.

Caitlin glanced over her shoulder to make certain that Sophie with her menacing microphone wasn't following them to get more footage for the news.

Maybe the interview Sophie had done with Matt would get edited out because of Mackenzie starting to cry, not being a picture-perfect baby at that moment.

Yes, okay, Matt had fielded the questions about his wife with slippery expertise, but would the average person watching the news realize that Matt never did say he was married, was the twins' father? Oh, forget it. She didn't have the energy to think about this. She just wanted to go home.

After luggage was collected, hugs were exchanged with the others from the group as well as promises to get together just as soon as their lives settled into sensible routines.

Marsha told Caitlin she'd telephone tomorrow, or maybe this *was* tomorrow for all she knew.

Madison and Mackenzie wailed their displeasure at being confined to the car seats during the entire drive to Caitlin's house.

"I fantasized about this moment." Caitlin raised her voice so Matt could hear her over the babies as they entered her living room. "You know, walking into my house carrying my baby, having her look around as though she knew she was finally home where she belonged and... Never mind. They're both so unhappy." She glanced at the ceiling. "I wonder if the plaster will crack from this noise. Gracious."

"Dry diapers and bottles are called for here. Let's do it, then I'll bring in your suitcase."

"Oh, Matt, you're as exhausted as I am, as the twins are. I can't ask you to stay and help me change and feed them."

"You're not asking, I'm volunteering. Don't argue the point. I don't have the energy to debate the subject."

A half hour later, the babies were changed, fed and wearing fresh sleepers taken from the dresser in the nursery. Caitlin and Matt tucked them into opposite ends of the crib. They wiggled a bit, then closed their eyes and slept.

"Oh, blessed silence," Caitlin said, then smiled up at Matt. "Look at them. They're here, Matt. They're honest-to-goodness here. Home. I don't believe it." She laughed. "I'll believe it the next time they wake up, that's for sure. Well, I'm going to take a leisurely bubble bath while I have the chance."

"I'll get your suitcase, then hit the road."

Matt strode from the room and Caitlin stood for another long moment gazing at the sleeping babies.

"Welcome home," she whispered. "I'm so very glad you're here, my darlings. I love you so much."

She turned and walked slowly from the room. Matt reentered the house and set Caitlin's suitcase by the front door.

"Well, I'm outta here," he said, not looking directly at her. "I'll get the second crib tomorrow and pick up some groceries for you. I'll phone you before I come over, to be certain it's a convenient time for you."

"Let me give you some money for the crib and food."

"Don't worry about it, Caitlin. We'll even up later." Matt paused. "So. We did it. We got those munchkins home safe and sound and... Hey, you know, if you need an extra set of hands just give me a shout and... No, I guess you won't do that, will you? Well, I'll pop in tomorrow with the crib and... Goodbye, Caitlin."

"Matt, wait." Caitlin closed the distance between them. "Thank you for everything. I don't have any idea how to express my gratitude for your help, for... All I can say is a simple thank-you knowing it isn't enough."

"I enjoyed every minute of it." He looked directly into Caitlin's eyes. "You know I did. Those girls own a chunk of my heart, always will, and you... Well, there's no sense in going there again, is there? I'll see you tomorrow."

Matt turned and left the house, closing the door behind him with a gentle click. Caitlin wrapped her hands around her elbows and stared at the door, aware of how very quiet it was, how empty somehow, despite the fact that two babies were sleeping down the hall. Aware of how much she already missed Matt MacAllister. Tears filled her eyes and she blinked them away, shaking her head in self-disgust.

"Go take a bubble bath, Caitlin," she said, starting across the room. "And while you're at it, get your act together."

During Caitlin's absence her neighbor, Stella, a widow in her mid-sixties, had collected Caitlin's mail, placed it on the desk in the bedroom she used for an office and watered the plants as needed.

After her very relaxing bath where she had actually been able to blank her mind, Caitlin checked on the still-sleeping twins, then stood staring at the pile of mail on her cluttered desk.

Forget it, she thought, she wasn't plowing through all this now. Her mother had made her promise to telephone when she, the mommy, arrived home and neither the new grandma nor the grandpa would care one iota what hour it was.

Caitlin's address book was, thank goodness, tucked safely in the top drawer of the desk, and moments later she was sitting in the chair and pressing the long list of numbers to make the international call. Caitlin's mother answered on the first ring.

With Paulo listening on an extension, Caitlin delivered her fantastic news. The three-way conversation was a babble of excited asking and answering of questions, sniffles of joy and the grandparents' heartfelt wish that they were there to see and hold the babies as well as give Caitlin a helping hand.

"When do you think you'll be able to visit?" Caitlin asked finally. "What is going on with your tests, Paulo?"

"Oh, nothing fancy," Paulo said. "I need double-bypass surgery, which is a walk in the park these days. What will hold up our getting on the plane is that it turns out I'm anemic and they are building me up before they operate. I'm afraid we can't put our finger on a date on the calendar at this point, sweetheart, so send us lots of pictures of our granddaughters."

"But you're going to be fine?" Caitlin said, frowning.

"As good as new," Paulo said.

"That's wonderful," she said. "I'll just have to be patient then, and wait until you two can make the trip."

"But how will you manage alone with two babies?" Olivia said. "As far as that goes, how did you manage on your own in China?"

"I had…I had help in China," Caitlin said quietly. "There was a man, Matt MacAllister, who is a friend of one of the couples and who knows all about babies and… Well, Matt was my…my partner, per se, in tending to the girls while we were over there.''

''I see,'' Caitlin's mother said slowly. ''And?''

''And…what?''

''Caitlin, I'm your mother. I know you as well as I know myself. Something changed in your voice when you mentioned Matt MacAllister's name. There's something you're not telling us.''

Oh, it's no biggie, Mom, Caitlin thought miserably. It's just the fact that she might very well have fallen in love with Matt, with the wrong man, while halfway around the world. But she wasn't about to tell her mother and Paulo that as they would only worry about her, and they had enough to deal with concerning Paulo's health.

''Caitlin?'' her mother said.

''What? Oh, I'm sorry, Mom. The something I'm not telling you is that I'm falling asleep sitting here because of jet lag. They told us to stay up as late as we could tonight to get back on schedule but… Anyway, you're up to date on my news. Exciting, isn't it? Almost unbelievable.''

Goodbyes were exchanged, more sniffles echoed across the telephone lines, then Caitlin hung up the receiver. She leaned back in the chair and sighed.

The sound of a crying baby reached Caitlin and she jumped to her feet, the addition of a second wailing infant causing her to run from the room and down the hall toward the nursery. She came to a halt next to the crib where the unhappy twins were voicing their displeasure at the top of their lungs.

"I'm here. Mommy is here," she said above the din as she scooped up Mackenzie. "Don't cry. Everything is under control."

And her nose was going to grow, Caitlin thought, placing Mackenzie on the changing table as Madison cried on. Just like Pinocchio.

Chapter Thirteen

Matt flung back the blankets and left the bed. As he strode toward the bathroom, each heavy footfall was accompanied by his earthy expletive.

What a lousy night's sleep that had been, he fumed as he stood under the stinging water in the shower moments later. He'd stayed up, per instructions, as late as possible the night before to hopefully conquer his jet lag. When he'd begun to nod off in his favorite recliner he had given up the battle and gone to bed.

Yeah, sure, he'd fallen right to sleep, only to jerk awake an hour later positive that he'd heard Mackenzie and Madison crying. That had proven to be part of the dream he'd been having about Caitlin and the twins. He'd repeated that performance two hours later, then two after that until he was so stressed his head was pounding and his stomach burning. Enough was enough.

So here he was, Matt mentally rambled on as he pulled on jeans and a knit shirt, all dressed and nowhere to go because it was 6:16 in the morning.

Toting a mug of freshly brewed coffee Matt settled in the recliner and glowered into space.

He missed Caitlin, he thought. He loved her, he missed her, he wanted to be with her instead of sitting here alone…and lonely. And he missed Mackenzie and Madison, too, damn it.

Matt took a sip of coffee and narrowed his eyes.

Look at the bright side, MacAllister, he told himself. Okay, he would…except what was it? There wasn't one bright and sunny thing about the fact that the woman he loved and who, yes, darn it, loved him in kind refused to allow him to be part of her present and future.

Okay, so he'd see Caitlin and the babies today when he delivered the crib and groceries. But even if he moved as slow as molasses, it wouldn't take him more than an hour to put the crib together. One crummy little hour. Hell.

If he even lasted long enough to get through that hour without exploding into a zillion pieces from tension-building frustration.

The store where he would buy the crib to match the other one didn't open until nine o'clock. There was no way on earth he could sit here that long without going straight out of his mind.

He would go to the hospital and kill some time, just wander into his office and see how things were with ole Homer at the helm. He'd make it clear he wasn't there to work, was just passing by and decided to say howdy. It wasn't a great plan but it was all he had.

Matt had only gotten about three feet from the elevator when his secretary, Linda, spotted him and rushed to stand in front of him, blocking his way. Linda was in her mid-forties but appeared haggard and thoroughly exhausted.

''What are you doing here so early?'' Matt said.

''I can't remember if I went home last night. Thank the stars you're back. This place is a zoo, Matt. Are you really standing before my very eyes or are you a figment of my imagination that has willed you to appear?''

''I'm here, but I'm not. What I mean is, I'm not reporting for duty. I just dropped by to say hello.''

''You can't leave again,'' Linda said, grasping one of Matt's hands with both of hers. ''We're in the midst of a crisis, a full-blown disaster, I tell you.''

''Where's Homer?''

"He had an emergency appendectomy yesterday morning, and no one is running this show. I swear, Matt, everything that could go wrong has gone wrong.

"Would you believe we have a man suing the hospital for emotional distress because they cut his shirt off in the E.R. to jump-start his heart? His wife gave him that shirt for their anniversary, and he's despondent that it was shredded.

"And there's some royal somebody in for heart surgery and he brought his own cook and the health department says no way is that guy cooking in the hospital kitchen.

"And a woman is having her attorney get a court order to allow her to have her poodle sleep with her in her hospital bed the night before her gall-bladder surgery.

"And—"

"Whoa. Halt. Stop," Matt said.

"But that's just the tip of the iceberg. There is a stack of files on your desk that you wouldn't believe."

"Okay, look. I'll donate a couple of hours and put out the worst of the fires, then I'm out of here, Linda. I have a baby crib and some groceries to buy, and I intend to do that."

"Which reminds me that I'm furious with you for not telling me you got married. Why keep it a secret, as well as your plans to adopt a baby from

China? I saw you on the news last night. Twins? They are so cute, Matt, but my feelings are hurt to think—''

''Things are not always what they seem to be,'' Matt said. ''I'll explain about the marriage and the twins later. Right now I need to get to work here, but I meant it when I said I'm only putting in a couple of hours.''

Just before nine o'clock that night Matt pulled in to Caitlin's driveway and turned off the ignition to the SUV. He rotated his neck back and forth in an attempt to loosen the tight muscles, then gave up the effort as futile. He chewed two antacid tablets, then got out of the vehicle.

Ridiculous day, he fumed, striding to the rear of the SUV. He hadn't had a thing to eat, his stomach was on fire, his head was holding a convention for bongo-drum players and he was many hours later getting to Caitlin's than he'd intended to be.

Matt opened the rear hatch of the vehicle and wrapped his arms around two packed-to-the-brim grocery bags.

Each time he'd reached for the phone to call Caitlin and tell her he hadn't forgotten his promise to get the crib and groceries, his hand had stilled. He'd been so afraid he'd call at the exact time when Caitlin was managing to take a nap because the twins were also sleeping.

Matt rang Caitlin's doorbell with his elbow, then cringed as he heard the chimes inside the house, envisioning the noise waking the babies, which would result, no doubt, in Caitlin popping him right in the chops.

"Who is it, please?" Caitlin's muffled voice asked from beyond the door.

"Matt."

"Matt who?"

"Caitlin, come on. I know you're probably upset with me because I didn't get here earlier, but I'm holding grocery bags, and if you keep me standing hcrc you're going to have a front porch that is decorated in melted raspberry sherbet."

A silent second ticked by, then two, then three.

"Caitlin?"

Matt heard the snap of the lock as it was released, then the door was opened to reveal a frowning Caitlin.

"Let me get the sherbet into the freezer, then I'll explain why I'm so late. Okay?"

Caitlin stepped back and swept one arm through the air. She didn't speak, nor did the stormy expression on her face soften one iota.

Matt entered the house and hurried to the kitchen. He placed the bags on the counter and began to unpack them, glancing at Caitlin as she sat down at the table.

"How are the twins?"

"Fine."

"Good. Did you get along all right today with the two of them?" he said, putting the sherbet in the freezer.

"Yes."

"Was it fun?"

"Yes."

"Do you think you could add a little more to this conversation than one-word answers, Caitlin?"

"No."

Matt shoved lettuce, tomatoes, cucumbers and bean sprouts into the refrigerator then crossed the room and sat down opposite Caitlin.

"Look, I'm really sorry I'm so late getting here. I started to call you a half-dozen times but never did it because I was afraid I'd wake you if you'd managed to catch a nap when the babies were sleeping. I fully intended to be here hours ago but—"

"Let me guess," Caitlin said, crossing her arms on the top of the table and leaning toward him. "You decided to stop by the hospital just to say hello, see if things were running smoothly without your expertise. And lo and behold, there was some kind of a crisis, or emergency, or whatever, that you just had to tend to while you were there. How am I doing, Matt? Have I hit the nail on its ever-famous head?"

"You're making it sound like I did something

totally unreasonable. Cripe, Caitlin, the guy who was covering for me had emergency surgery and things were piling up and—''

''And nobody could fix it all but you,'' Caitlin said, getting to her feet. ''And, of course, that hospital, what you do there, is far more important than buying a second crib and filling my Mother Hubbard cupboards.''

''That's not true,'' Matt said, lunging to his feet.

His chair fell over and toppled to the floor with a crash. He and Caitlin froze, straining their ears for the sound of…

Mackenzie began to cry. Then Madison began to cry.

''You—'' Caitlin pointed at him ''—are a dead man.''

She spun around and stomped out of the kitchen.

Matt set his chair back into place. ''You're doing just dandy so far, MacAllister. Men have been murdered for waking a sleeping baby and I woke up two. I'm scoring points all over the map.''

Maybe he could redeem himself, he thought, hurrying after Caitlin. He'd step in and lend a hand with the now-wailing babies, be useful, needed. Oh, yeah, that was it. He could show Caitlin that she needed him there to help her, if she'd forget for a second that he was the one who woke the girls in the first place.

When Matt arrived at the open doorway of the

nursery, the twins were quieting and the clowns hanging from the mobile were dancing in a circle to the lilting lullaby. A night-light cast a soft, golden glow over the room.

"Shh," Caitlin was saying. "You're all right. Mommy is right here. That was a loud noise, wasn't it? But everything is fine. Go to sleep, my darlings. Mommy is here."

And so is Daddy, Matt's mind yelled.

"May I see them?" he said quietly. "Please?"

Caitlin turned her head to look at him, then finally nodded. Matt went to the crib and stared at the babies who had drifted back to sleep.

"Hello, little munchkins. I missed seeing you guys today, I really did." He shifted his gaze to Caitlin, his heart seeming to skip a beat when he found her looking directly into his eyes. "I missed you, too, Caitlin. I know I blew it by being so late getting here but... Ah, Caitlin, I love you so damn much."

"Don't." She shook her head as her eyes filled with tears.

Caitlin hurried from the room and Matt followed slowly behind her. In the living room he found her standing by the sofa, her hands wrapped protectively around her elbows.

"Caitlin," Matt said, stopping across the room from her, "we can have it all, don't you see, if you'll only give me a chance to—"

"To repeat what happened today?" she said, tears spilling unnoticed onto her cheeks. "Over and over and over again? Promises made, promises broken? No. I grew up with that kind of heartache, watched my mother be destroyed by inches by it, too. I won't do that to myself, not again, nor will I allow it to happen to my daughters.

"Leave us alone, Matt. It isn't going to work between us, not in a million years. It's too painful to have you here, in my home." A sob caught in her throat. "I might be in love with you, I don't know, but I don't like how you view life, your priorities, what you believe is more important than…" She shook her head as tears choked off her words.

"But—"

"No. No, no, no."

Matt's shoulders slumped and an achy sensation gripped his throat, making it impossible to speak.

This was it? he thought. The end? He would never see Caitlin Cunningham again? He wouldn't be here to watch the twins learn to crawl, then take those first, wondrous wobbling steps? He'd never hear those little girls call him Daddy? Oh, God, no. He couldn't bear the thought of a future without the woman he loved, without his Caitlin. Without his family.

"I…" Matt started, then realized he didn't know

what to say as a jumble of tangled, confusing thoughts flooded his mind.

"Please go," Caitlin said.

"Yeah," he said, nodding. "Okay. But I intend to put the crib together first, Caitlin. You can go to your bedroom or whatever. I'll work here in the living room and you can pull the crib into the nursery in the morning."

Caitlin nodded jerkily, dashed the tears from her cheeks, then left the room. Matt watched her go, and with a weary sigh headed outside to bring in the boxes containing the crib and mattress.

An hour later Matt shut his toolbox, then wound the knob on the clown mobile that he'd bought to match the other one. To the sound of the pretty song that he had once held Caitlin in his arms and danced to, he left the house, closing the door on his happiness.

A week later Matt slid into the booth in a busy café and immediately raised both hands in a gesture of peace as he looked at his glowering twin sister, Noel.

"I know, I know, I'm guilty as sin," he said.

"Got it in one," Noel said, narrowing her eyes. "You've been avoiding the whole family since you returned from China, haven't returned our calls or… For crying out loud, Matt, we saw you on the news last week. I am the official MacAllister representative, buster, and you're not leaving this restaurant until you tell me what's going on.''

"Can we order lunch first?" Matt said, attempting to produce a smile that fizzled.

"Make it snappy," Noel said.

They ordered hamburgers and fries, then Noel tapped the fingers of one hand impatiently on the table. "Speak," she said. "And this better be good. Oh, by the way, you look like hell.''

"I haven't been sleeping well. Plus I've been putting in long hours at the hospital and—''

"Wait a minute," Noel said. "You're not even supposed to be back at work yet...according to Bud's orders.''

"It can't be helped. The guy who was taking my place had his appendix out and... I've been trying to put in decent hours at the hospital, Noel, but every night when I get ready to leave something comes up that needs my attention. Caitlin was right about me. I'm not fit to be a husband and father. I can't have it all and it's tearing me to shreds.''

Their lunches were put in front of them and ignored.

"Back up, back up," Noel said. "Start at the top. There's nothing we can't solve if we put our genius-level minds together.''

"Not this time. It's hopeless. *I'm* hopeless. And, oh, God, Noel, I love Caitlin Cunningham and those babies so much I can't even begin to express it to you in words. They're…my life, my…" He shook his head.

Noel covered one of Matt's hands with one of hers on the top of the table.

"Start at the beginning," she said gently. "You decided to tag along on the trip to China with Bud and Marsha and…" She gave Matt's hand a little squeeze. "And?"

And Matt began to talk, pouring out his heart to his sister, his twin. They had been more than just sister and brother since they had been born on that same day thirty-two years before. They were best friends.

But even Noel hadn't known Matt's deepest secret of why he was so driven to succeed in his career, the inner need to be the best at something just as all the MacAllisters were.

"Oh, honey," Noel said, shaking her head as Matt revealed the truth. "We've always been so close. Yet you kept this churning inside you."

"I told Caitlin this while we were in China," Matt said. "She made me realize that I didn't need to be Mr. Sunshine all of the time, plus the fact that I needed to change the pattern of how I was living. No, correct that. Not living…just existing."

Noel nodded.

Matt continued his story, his voice often raspy with emotion.

"I was going to be a macho MacAllister, fight

the toughest battle of my life and win, prove to Caitlin that I could change, that I was worthy of her love, of being her husband and the father to our daughters.

"But, Noel? I didn't win. I won't win. Not now. Not in the future. Not ever. Because this past week has shown me that Caitlin is right about me. I can't change. God knows I tried, but…" Matt's voice trailed off.

"You've created a monster."

"And his name is Matt MacAllister," he said with a sharp bark of laughter that held absolutely no humor.

"No, sweetie," Noel said. "Its name is Mercy Hospital."

"What?" he said, obviously confused.

"Oh, Matt, don't you see?" she said, leaning toward him. "It's the people at Mercy who need to change. They're not willing to allow you to delegate. Can you reprogram all of them? Of course not. But don't you dare say that *you* can't change your ways."

Matt picked up a very cold fry, looked at it for a long moment, then tossed it back onto the plate.

"You're dealing in semantics, Noel," he said, leaning back in the booth. "The bottom line is still the same. It's hopeless. I've lost Caitlin. I've lost my baby girls."

Noel shook her head. "You're wrong. What you

need to do is right there in front of your nose, Matt.''

''That's news to me,'' he said, frowning. ''Would you care to share this what-any-idiot-should-be-able-to-see answer to my dilemma?''

''No. I'm sorry, Matt, but no. You've got to figure it out on your own. It has to come from your mind, your heart, your very soul so that you own it, make it truly yours.

''I'll give you a clue, though, because you're a man and your species is generally dense.''

''I used to like you, Noel.'' Matt sighed. ''Okay, lay it on me. The clue.''

''Okay. Here it is. Take another look at the gift you received from Grandpa.''

''The scale? My gift didn't have a hidden meaning like so many of the others he gave to his grandchildren. It's a beautiful object, but it doesn't have a message I'm supposed to figure out.''

''Doesn't it?'' Noel slid out of the booth, came around the table and kissed Matt on the forehead. ''I love you, my brother. Go look at the scale again.''

Chapter Fourteen

At ten o'clock that night Matt leaned back in the chair behind his desk at the hospital with a weary sigh. He squeezed his temples between the fingers of one hand, hoping the pressure would lessen the pain of his throbbing headache. It didn't.

Matt got to his feet and crossed the room to retrieve his suit coat from the clothes tree in the corner. As he slipped on the jacket his gaze fell on the antique scale that was still sitting on the bookcase where he had placed it to humor Homer Holmes.

Well, Matt thought wearily, if he'd been that accommodating for a nerdy, fussbudget attorney, he at least owed Noel the courtesy of *looking* at the scale again…which was a total waste of time.

Matt scooped the two coins off the left tray of the scale, dropped them into his pocket, then picked up the scale and left the office.

At home, Matt set the scale on the table next to his favorite chair and laid the two coins by it.

When his grandfather had given him the gift of the scale, he mused, the two coins had been held in place in the left tray by a narrow strip of tape. He'd removed it when he took the scale to his office, leaving both coins in that tray.

Matt placed one coin in the left tray, then hesitated before doing the same with the other one. He stared intently at the scale, the coin in his hand, then the scale again.

Every muscle in his body seemed to tense and he had to remind himself to breathe. Acutely aware that his hand was trembling, Matt put the second coin in the right tray, causing the saucer-shaped disks to move, then still in perfect side-by-side balance.

"Oh, my God," Matt said aloud. "Noel was right."

There *had* been a message connected to the gift that his grandfather had given him, he thought, his mind racing. There was the answer right in front him. Balance. That was what was sorely missing in his existence. An equal and healthy balance between his career and his personal life. Noel was a very smart woman. And his grandfather? Oh, what a wise and wonderful man was Robert MacAllister.

"Caitlin and the babies," Matt said, his voice ringing with emotion. He gently touched the coin in the left-hand tray with one fingertip, then switched his gaze to the other coin. "My job at Mercy. In proper balance."

You've created a monster. Its name is Mercy Hospital.

Noel's words echoed suddenly in Matt's mind, causing his heart to race. Time lost meaning as Matt continued to stare at the scale.

Very early the next morning Matt telephoned Noel.

"Do you know what time it is?" she said, nearly yelling.

"I'm sorry I woke you," Matt said, "but I have to talk to you. I need your help, Noel."

Three days later in the early afternoon Caitlin sat cross-legged on the floor of her living room next to a blanket where the twins were on their tummies, picking up, then discarding, a variety of brightly colored toys. A yellow envelope was in her lap and she was staring at a photograph that was one of many in the envelope containing the developed pictures of the trip to China.

Tears stung her eyes as she continued to gaze at the photograph she was clutching.

There they all were, Caitlin thought, swallowing past the lump in her throat. This picture was taken at the celebration dinner on the last night in China. There they all were—Matt, Caitlin, Mackenzie and Madison. They were dressed in the traditional red, and they were all smiling.

Like a happy family.

"Oh, Matt," she said, then sniffled. "There's nowhere left for me to hide from the truth. I love you, Matt MacAllister, so very, very much. If only… No, I'm not going down the 'if only' road. There's nothing to be gained from that. But, oh, if only…"

The doorbell rang and Caitlin nearly cheered aloud that something had pulled her back to reality and reason. She got to her feet and hurried to the door.

"Hello," a woman said, smiling, after Caitlin opened the door.

"Hello," Caitlin replied, producing a small smile. "May I help you?"

"You don't know me, Caitlin, but I feel as though I know you. And Mackenzie and Madison. I'm Noel. Matt's sister. May I come in for a second?"

"Oh…well…sure," Caitlin said, stepping back to allow Noel to enter the house.

"There they are," Noel said, laughing in delight. "Oh, Caitlin, your daughters are sensational, just adorable."

"Thank you."

"I hope you don't mind that I brought them a little gift," Noel said, handing Caitlin a glossy pink bag.

"This is very kind of you. Please, sit down."

"Thanks," Noel said, glancing at her watch as she settled onto the sofa.

Caitlin sat down on the opposite end and took the tissue out of the top of the bag. She pulled out two pink T-shirts and two pink seersucker bib overalls.

"Oh, thank you, Noel. This is so lovely of you, especially since you don't even know me."

"Like I said," Noel said, looking quickly at her watch again, "I feel as though I know you and the babies. Matt told me all about you three."

"Really?" Caitlin said, making a production out of folding the new clothes, smoothing them, then placing them on the coffee table. "How...how is Matt?" She turned her head slowly to look at Noel.

"Oh, you know," Noel said, flipping one hand in the air. "Matt is Matt."

Caitlin frowned. "In other words, he's back to his old routine of working ungodly hours at the hospital."

"I was thinking more in the terms of his being

a handsome, loving, caring and sharing, thoughtful and kind, intelligent man.''

''Who is working ungodly hours at the hospital again, right?''

Noel looked at her watch. ''Oh, my. Oh, my. Look at the time. I don't mean to be a rude guest but there's a press conference starting in about a minute or so and it's going to be televised. Would you mind if I watched it?''

''No, I don't mind.'' Caitlin picked up the remote control from the coffee table and pressed a button to bring the television to life. ''What channel do you want?''

''The Ventura station. This is a press conference being held here.''

''Oh,'' Caitlin said, then found the proper station. ''I'll go heat some bottles for the babies while you're watching this.''

''No,'' Noel said none too quietly.

Caitlin jerked in surprise at her visitor's outburst.

''What I mean is—'' Noel beamed ''—I really believe you'll find this press conference very… informative.'' She glanced at the babies. ''Your sweeties are content at the moment.''

''Well, okay,'' Caitlin said, deciding that Matt's sister was a tad strange.

''Here we go,'' Noel said as the words *special bulletin* appeared on the television screen.

The next image was of an attractive woman speaking into a handheld microphone.

"This is Sophie Spencer," the woman said, "reporting to you live outside of Mercy Hospital here in Ventura. Matt MacAllister, who is a household name in our city, has called a press conference that will begin any minute now. We have no idea what this pertains to."

Caitlin's eyes widened, her gaze riveted on the screen. Mackenzie began to whine.

"I'll get her," Noel said, moving to the blanket and picking up the fussing infant. "Not now, kiddo. Your mommy is busy."

"I don't need to watch this news conference," Caitlin said, rising. "I'll go warm the bottles."

"Caitlin Cunningham," Noel yelled, "sit back down on that sofa and don't move."

Mackenzie began to cry and Noel patted her on the back.

"Noel..." Caitlin said, obviously having had enough of Noel's weird behavior.

"Look," Noel said, pacing back and forth in an attempt to pacify the unhappy Mackenzie. "I'm doing a lousy job here, but I don't exactly do this for a living, for heaven's sake. Please, Caitlin, just do it. Please? Sit down and listen to what Matt has to say."

Caitlin sank back down on the sofa with a sigh of defeat. Matt MacAllister was about to arrive smack-dab in her living room, Caitlin thought frantically. She would hear the rich timbre of his voice, drink in the sight of his wide shoulders, his thick, auburn hair, those mesmerizing fudge-sauce-colored eyes of his. He would no doubt smile at some point while making the announcement about whatever it was he was making the announcement about and…

Madison began to cry.

"Oh, dear," Caitlin said, landing back in reality with a thud.

"Fear not," Noel said, heading in the direction she assumed would lead her to the kitchen. "I can handle this. Two bottles coming right up, little cuties."

"And here is Matt MacAllister now," Sophie said as a door of the hospital opened behind her.

There were three other reporters besides Sophie, who were stringers for the national news stations. Their bosses would determine whether what was covered should be added to the evening newscast. Four microphones were tilted in Matt's direction.

Oh, look at him, Caitlin thought. He was so handsome. But he appeared to be exhausted, had dark smudges under his eyes.

Noel returned to the living room, plunked Mackenzie in Caitlin's lap and handed her a bottle, then scooped up Madison from the floor. She tucked Madison next to her on the sofa, retrieved Mackenzie from Caitlin and popped bottles into mouths.

"Matt fed them that way on the plane one time," Caitlin said, "so I could get some sleep."

"MacAllisters know their stuff when it comes to tending to babies," Noel said. "Shh. Listen to Matt."

"Thank you for coming, ladies and gentlemen," Matt said. "The board of directors and I agreed that this is the most efficient way to get this known. I have," Matt went on, "turned in my resignation letter for the position of public-relations director at Mercy Hospital."

"What?" Caitlin whispered, inching to the edge of the sofa and staring at the television with wide eyes.

"Shh," Noel said.

"I've enjoyed my many years here at Mercy," Matt said, "but it's time for a change, time for *me* to change. Not just talk about it, but actually do it, and I am. There is more to life than a fancy title, a record of excellence and a plush office inside a tall building."

"What are your plans, Matt?" Sophie asked.

"I'm going to open my own public-relations firm," he said. "It won't be the biggest, nor the most well-known operation, but it will allow me to have a proper balance in my existence between work and my personal life.

"My replacement here at Mercy will be Homer Holmes, who is a fine attorney and who will do a superb job of stepping into my shoes. He's already had some experience here while I was away recently."

"I don't believe this," Caitlin said, flattening her hands on her cheeks.

"Shh," Noel said.

"Matt," Sophie said, "I know that all of Ventura wishes you the very best in your new endeavor and I'm certain your public-relations agency will be a huge success."

"Thank you, Sophie," Matt said, smiling.

"One more question," Sophie said. "There seems to be some confusion about whether or not you are married and are the daddy of those adorable adopted babies we saw you with at the airport. Could you clear that up for our viewers? Do you have a family, or not? Are you a husband and father?"

Caitlin's breath caught and she pressed trembling fingertips against her lips.

"I'm not avoiding answering your question, Sophie," Matt said, "nor do I mean to sound mysterious, or whatever. It's just that I honestly don't know. I'm not the person to answer that." He shifted his gaze from Sophie to look directly into the camera. "Caitlin? If Noel came through for me, and she always has in the past, then you're watching this. Am I married, Caitlin? Do I have two beautiful daughters?''

Caitlin extended one hand toward the television as tears filled her eyes. "Yes. Oh, yes, Matt."

"Oh, jeez," Noel said, sniffling, "this is so romantic I'm falling apart." She reached past the babies and took a piece of paper from her purse that was on the floor next to the sofa.

"Here." She handed Caitlin the paper. "This is Matt's cell-phone number."

Caitlin snatched up the telephone receiver on the end table next to her and punched in the numbers. She heard it ring in her ear and on the television screen at the same time. Matt retrieved the phone from his jacket pocket but didn't speak as he pressed it to his ear.

"Hello, Mr. MacAllister," Caitlin said, smiling through her tears.

She replaced the receiver on the base.

"That's it?" Noel said. "You didn't tell him that—"

"Shh," Caitlin said.

"Yes," Matt said, punching one fist in the air.

"Yes...what?" Sophie said. "Matt, I'm still confused."

"Gotta go," Matt said, grinning. "I'll call you later, Sophie, and give you the details. Bye."

Matt disappeared off the screen and the camera zoomed in on Sophie.

"This is Sophie Spencer," she said, laughing, "a confused Sophie Spencer, reporting live from Mercy Hospital. We'll give you more details on this story as we get them. We now return you to your regular programming."

"She thinks *she's* confused," Noel said. "Caitlin, does your saying 'Hello, Mr. MacAllister' to Matt mean we're getting a happy ending here?"

Caitlin pressed the remote to turn off the television and smiled at Noel.

"Oh, yes, very happy and very forever," Caitlin said. "Matt understood what I meant by my saying what I did. He's on his way over here right now."

"I'm gone," Noel said. "The babies are asleep. Let's get them into their cribs." She frowned. "'Hello, Mr. MacAllister'? I just don't get it."

The twins were tucked into their beds, Noel hugged Caitlin, who thanked Matt's sister for her wonderful performance, then Noel rushed out the door.

Five minutes after Noel left, Matt pulled in to the driveway, patted his suit coat pocket to be certain once again that the rings he'd bought in China were safely there and seconds later was sprinting toward the front door of Caitlin's house. She flung open the door, her eyes brimming with tears and a lovely smile on her face. Matt stepped into the room, pushed the door closed, then framed her face in his hands.

"Hello," he said, his voice husky with emotion and his dark brown eyes glistening. "Hello, Mrs. MacAllister."

He lowered his head and kissed her, softly, reverently, lovingly. It was a kiss that sealed their commitment to a life to be spent together, in proper balance.

They were Mr. and Mrs. MacAllister, father and mother to Mackenzie and Madison, husband and wife, from now until forever.

* * * * *

*Be sure to watch for another
MacAllister romance, coming only to
Silhouette Special Edition in 2004.*

Nora's extraordinary Donovan family is back!

#1 *New York Times* bestselling author

NORA ROBERTS

Captivated

The Donovans remain one of Nora Roberts's most unforgettable
families. For along with their irresistible appeal they've inherited
some rather remarkable gifts from their Celtic ancestors. In this
classic story Nash Kirkland falls under the bewitching spell of
mysterious Morgana Donovan.

Available in February at your favorite retail outlet.

Where love comes alive™

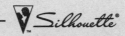

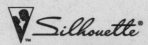 **Silhouette®**

COMING NEXT MONTH

SPECIAL EDITION

#1585 EXPECTING!—Susan Mallery
Merlyn County Midwives

Hearth and home were essential to Hannah Wisham Bingham, and she'd returned to Merlyn County, pregnant and alone, for the support of community and old friends. What she hadn't expected was the help of her *very* grown-up, career-minded best friend, Eric Mendoza. But Hannah had the perfect job for the sexy executive—as dad!

#1586 MacGOWAN MEETS HIS MATCH—Annette Broadrick
Secret Sisters

Searching for her long-lost family had led Jenna Craddock to the Scottish Highlands...and to Sir Ian MacGowan. The grumpy British intelligence agent hired Jenna to be his secretary—never expecting the high-spirited beauty to be the woman he never knew he needed. But could Ian convince Jenna his intentions were true?

#1587 THE BLACK SHEEP HEIR—Crystal Green
Kane's Crossing

As the newfound illegitimate son of the powerful Spencer clan, Connor Langley was forced to choose between proving his loyalty to his new family by getting Lacey Vedae to give up her coveted Spencer land, or devoting himself to the sweet and vulnerable Lacey, who was slowly invading his jaded heart.

#1588 THEIR BABY BOND—Karen Rose Smith

She wanted a child, not a husband. So Tori Phillips opted for adoption. And she unexpectedly found support for her decision from her teenage crush, Jake Galeno. Jake became her confidant through the whole emotional process...acting almost as if he wanted a family, too.

#1589 BEAUTICIAN GETS MILLION-DOLLAR TIP!—Arlene James
The Richest Gals in Texas

Struggling hairstylist Valerie Blunt had a lot on her mind—well, mainly, the infuriatingly attractive Fire Marshal Ian Keene. Ian set fires in Valerie whenever he was near, but the little matter of the cool million she inherited made their relationship a million times more difficult!

#1590 A PERFECT PAIR—Jen Safrey

Josey St. John was made for motherhood, and in search of the perfect husband. Her best friend, Nate Bennington, believed he could never be a family man. But Josey soon realized it was Nate she wanted. Could she prove to Nate his painful past wouldn't taint their future as a family?

SSECNM1203